GAIN TO LOSE

Dr Sheela Nambiar MD is a practising obstetrician gynaecologist and a fitness and lifestyle consultant. She holds a certification from the National Association of Fitness Certification (NAFC), USA.

She has her obstetric practice in Ooty and has a wellness/fitness program called Training For Life (TFL) which she uses as an extension of her medical practice. She also owns and runs the TFL fitness studio in Nungambakkam, Chennai.

She can be reached at:
Facebook: *www.facebook.com/tfl.trainingforlife?ref=tn_tnmn*
Blog: *sheelanambiar.wordpress.com*
Twitter: *@drsheelanambiar*

By the same author

Get Size Wise
Training for Life for the Indian Woman

GAIN TO LOSE

An Essential Guide to Losing Fat by Gaining Muscle

Dr Sheela Nambiar

RUPA

Published by
Rupa Publications India Pvt Ltd 2015
7/16, Ansari Road, Daryaganj
New Delhi 110002

Sales centres:
Allahabad Bengaluru Chennai
Hyderabad Jaipur Kathmandu
Kolkata Mumbai

While every effort has been made to verify the authenticity of the
information contained in this book, it is not intended as a substitute for
medical consultation with a physician. The publisher and the author are
in no way liable for the use of the information contained in this book.

ISBN: 978-81-291-3755-5

First impression 2015

10 9 8 7 6 5 4 3 2 1

The moral right of the author has been asserted.

This book is dedicated to all the women I have treated, counselled, trained or taught over the years, who have allowed me an insight into their lives.

CONTENTS

PROLOGUE

After my first book *Get Size Wise*, I did several interviews and talks with various women's groups for and about the book. Most of the questions orbited around the usual, 'What is the best way to lose weight?', 'What happens when you stop exercising?' and other such subjects. One perceptive journalist asked me a question, one I had asked myself several times before writing and publishing my first book. She asked me if the title of the book *Get Size Wise*, sounded a bit limiting in terms of the need for a good figure alone. She said it seemed a bit narrow when the book obviously took a larger, more holistic look at the importance of well-being for women. This thought did occur to me, but here is the thing. *Size* is a critical issue with most women. The use of the word, I hoped, would attract the reader to pick up the book in the first place. Thereafter, the content of the book would reveal that one needs to, literally, **get wise about one's size** and take a good look at the larger picture. This was done because:

» **Size should not be a limiting factor** in any way. Being large should not prevent you from starting an exercise programme or wanting to look good and get healthy.
» Size remains a **visual perspective** and your body's

dimensions. Thighs measuring twenty inches give no indication of whether the thighs are muscular and strong or flabby and primarily fat.

» As **muscle weighs more than fat**, a muscular body may weigh more than a body on the fatter side while being the same size. Weighing oneself on the scale, therefore, also needs to be done while keeping this fact in perspective.

» One needs to work towards **a size which showcases quality**. It must have more muscle mass, with stronger, more flexible muscles, and a better cardiovascular and musculoskeletal system.

» Lastly, the **focus should be on fitness** and improving the quality of their body with one that has more muscle and less fat. This takes away unnecessary attention from weight or size.

Whoever created these sizes anyway? The fashion industry certainly did. This was perhaps done in order to simply standardize clothing. It does not mean you have to be a certain size. Body proportions vary infinitely among women.

My last book and this one as well are about one's physical well-being. This book helps you understand ways to get healthier by applying the right workout techniques, which result in fat loss and help you get into shape. I certainly have gone beyond the physical body in the book with discussions revolving around the psychology behind the impetus to exercise and lose weight. This is simply because one cannot disengage the physical from the emotional and mental. They are intertwined. This appears more so in women.

I also believe that women like to look good, thanks to evolutionary reason. Looking good makes them feel confident. As an obstetrician and gynaecologist (obgyn), and a fitness and lifestyle consultant working primarily with women, I have observed that when a woman starts to see positive physical changes, she develops a positive frame of mind. She is more receptive to change in other areas. This seems to be the window of opportunity for the consultant to step in to guide her positively to look at the bigger picture. She finds it easier to adapt and willing to go the extra mile because she has already started believing in herself and gained confidence. She is more willing and ready to evolve; in fact, it almost comes naturally to her.

This is very different from preying on the insecurities of women. It does not bode well to tell them they are not good enough, or slim enough or sexy enough. Women then get lured by the onslaught of profitable products like fat burners, cosmetic surgery, supplements and so on to fix these problems. This approach is counter-productive and makes women feel less confident and more insecure. This leads to temporary outward changes. The key word here is temporary. Regaining weight subsequent to weight loss then is a natural occurrence when contentious measures are followed.

At the opposite end of the spectrum are those influencing women to focus only on the spiritual and disconnect from the physical body. This is supposedly done in an effort to evolve to be a better human without any focus on the physical body. This almost implies that the physical body is not important and it is only the mind that matters.

I beg to differ entirely from these approaches. The human body is an extraordinary piece of architecture that we must respect and revere. It's hard to tell a woman who is overweight, uncomfortable with her body experiencing pain and disease that her physical body does not matter, given that that is the cause of her anguish. If one can help her overcome the physical discomfort, then the emotional journey becomes easier and more gratifying.

This book is also, on the surface, about physical appearance, but not entirely about this facet.

It is based on well-researched findings that when one builds or gains muscle, the body's basal metabolic rate or BMR increases (however marginally), leading to more calories being burnt even at rest. Weight training to increase muscle mass therefore, is key to maintaining a firm, strong body that serves its purpose of being functional, looking good and staying strong.

Gaining something is so much more psychologically reassuring than losing something. The book, thus, evolved to create a sense of reward and incentive from regular exercise with its innumerable benefits (besides the physical).

Gaining muscle is also not really a priority for women, specifically Indian women. It so happens that **gaining muscle is key to losing fat and enhancing several physiological processes in the body**. Aside from losing fat, getting stronger and looking better, gaining muscle improves the very functionality of the body.

» It improves healing and recovery following a surgery or disease.
» It helps deal better with diseases like diabetes, even resulting in a decrease in the medication required in the management of blood sugars.
» Pregnancy, labour and childbirth are demanding

occasions for a woman. Stronger, better muscles see her through these times easily.

» Getting back in shape following delivery, while handling the baby, besides the countless other chores that await her, is simpler when she is already fit and familiar with exercise.

» Loss of balance, falls and injury are more common when you have poor muscle strength to support, balance and carry you through day-to-day activities.

» Training with weights prevents the loss of muscle that typically follows ageing. Osteoporosis, primarily a woman's disease, is prevented and treated with weight training to build muscle and subsequently strengthen tendons, ligaments and bones.

While all the above seem to be purely physical benefits, the psychological benefits of getting stronger are immense and largely unappreciated. Fear of falling down that plagues many older (and sometimes younger, overweight) women stems from not having developed the strength in the right muscles. The increase in self-confidence that arises from the increase in physical strength cannot be underestimated.

Overall, weight training has huge benefits, including building muscle mass and strength. My intention in this book is to bring home this reality. It also stems from my own experience with training women. Those women who focus purely on cardio to lose *weight* (which in this case is a combination of fat and muscle), gain it back rapidly if they stop for a couple of weeks. Weight training to build muscle in addition to cardio, however, seems to prevent this rapid weight gain. The increase in muscle mass alters the body's physiology and capacity to burn fat. It alters the body's set-point. They also begin to view fitness very differently once weight training becomes a part of their routine. They are so much more confident, introspective and likely to listen to their bodies. There is substantial evidence emerging now indicating that Indians inherently have a lower muscle mass, making them more susceptible to obesity, diabetes and many other problems.

Most women begin with using very light weights, one and two kilos at the most. The usual contention being, 'I will become masculine' (more on that later). Understanding that one needs to increase the resistance (weight used) to improve and increase muscle mass dawns on them as they continue to train. Then they begin to want to lift heavier weights. They want to feel stronger and more confident.

In my younger days I was a cardio queen myself. I much preferred running on the treadmill, teaching step class, walking, cycling, and other such exercises. Age (and hopefully wisdom) has taught me that my body needs other things as well. Strength training and yoga take priority now. I love the pure Zen of lifting the barbell and putting it down. The thoughtfulness it requires, the power it generates. It produces a high that's very different from a runner's high. One that nonetheless is exhilarating and highly rewarding.

I hope that reading this book will encourage more women to take up weight training seriously. I hope they get fitter, not just to gain muscle and lose fat but to improve the overall quality of their bodies. As a natural progression, I hope they feel empowered, charged with positive energy and ready to deal with the other vicissitudes of life.

HOW TO USE THIS BOOK

This book is for someone who is interested in understanding her body and is willing to spend a little time reading about it. Someone for whom fitness is not one dimensional, or merely about looking slim.

Several chapters in the book go about explaining the various ways in which fat is burnt while building muscle. I even have a little story about Fluffy, the Fat Cell and his journey through our body.

Some chapters describe the importance of muscles, their structure and functioning, as well as the problems one faces when they have imbalanced muscles or less muscle mass and so on.

Some of the information may seem very technical. I have tried to simplify it and keep it interesting. I hope I have achieved that. I felt it was my responsibility to give you some sound, scientific information as well. I am quite sure my savvy reader will plunge right in and appreciate it.

Other chapters deal with subjects related to fitness and weight training and how to sustain a disciplined lifestyle. They are derived mainly from my own experiences with women, my personal understanding of the issues and the various research papers I have been swamped under over the last year trying to make sense of everything myself.

I have covered some basics about food on the chapters concerning fat, carbohydrates and protein. Food and nutrition are too vast to be explained in one book. The basics are available in my first book *Get Size Wise*.

Fitness is a vast and exciting subject. There is some fascinating research that comes out that keeps us motivated and experimenting all the time. There are also very definite rules and regulations for exercise that have held good for many decades. I have clearly delineated these principles through the book. Some rules, however, change over time. For instance, the concept of doing High-Intensity Interval Training (HIIT) for fat loss rather than long-duration low-intensity cardio is fairly new.

The importance of increasing muscle mass with weight training has gained momentum over the last decade. This is what I have tried to reiterate in this book.

The last few chapters explain sequences of the exercises you should do. They are explained with pictures, but if you are a beginner, I implore you to seek professional help.

I do hope that in the chapter dedicated to Frequently Asked Questions (FAQs) about weight training, I have answered the most common doubts women face about the subject.

The last chapter 'Wabi Sabi' is a charming philosophy for life.

1

THE BOILING FROG

We Adapt

I am certain most of you have heard of the *Boiling Frog Syndrome*. Dreadful as it sounds, it is an interesting theory. I am not sure who performed this experiment or why, but here is how the story goes:

Put a frog in boiling water and it jumps out immediately. Put it in water which is of room temperature and increase the temperature gradually, and the frog does not jump out. Instead, it dies when the water gets too hot.

The frog, in room temperature water, apparently can adjust its body temperature to the gradually increasing temperature of the surrounding water. It acclimatizes. However, when the water has reached boiling point, it has no energy left to jump out having used much of that valuable energy to adjust its body temperature to the rising temperature of the water.

Acclimatization is a great compliance tactic and is usually, but not always, a good thing.

This little story is analogous to the *slow weight gain* in our own lives. As we age, we gain fat. It is almost a certainty. We all adjust to the changes that come about gradually, without clearly registering that we are in fact adjusting to our (not necessarily better) environment and new status (the hotter frog).

It happens progressively. Two, five and ten kilos a year. We adapt beautifully to the excess baggage. We get used to carrying around the extra weight. We buy new clothes to contain the widening waistline. We move less as the discomfort increases. We devise strategies to accommodate our newfound lack of fitness and wellness. We buy better and fancier cars, use escalators instead of the stairs, use more comfortable seats and beds. We play less, preferring instead to watch TV or surf the Internet. We invest in the latest time saving devices and gadgets in order to save us the effort of physical work.

Our jobs support us. We are seated most of the day, eyes glued to an inanimate monitor, talking to people, signing papers, writing, talking endlessly on the telephone, stressed out, anxious, multitasking for the most part.

We have the food to go with the lifestyle. Mindless, calorie-laden food while at work, which is eaten without registering what goes in. Perhaps from a hotel nearby or the office canteen. The choices of cuisine are astounding. Each option richer than the next to enhance flavour. Then, there are the meetings, dinners, conferences, conventions with the wining and dining. Every such situation is yet another opportunity to eat and drink wildly and indiscriminately. We stumble along, convincing ourselves that this is just what we do. Such is life.

We develop lifestyle-related diseases like diabetes and hypertension. We cope with medication. After all, isn't that what the medicines are for? Our blood reports spell gloomy predictions, inviting more medication to keep the high cholesterol in check. We make the necessary excuses. We have the master health check-up which only increases the ominous prophesies and ensures more expenditure with drugs and an occasional trip to the fat farm to lose some unwanted kilos (which of course promptly pile right back on when we start living in the real world!). We consider bariatric surgery. The stress is too much and we see the shrink. We get on to the anti-depressants. So many choices!

WE ADAPT!

Just like the frog that adjusts its body temperature and spends precious energy adapting to its surrounding, we adapt. We spend a lot of energy, time and money doing so. At the end of it, we have no energy left to actually get out of the awful situation. It is almost a lost cause.

PREVENT THE WEIGHT GAIN TO BEGIN WITH!

Like the frog thrown into boiling water in the first place, if we react promptly to weight gain, the whole narrative changes.

- » We can choose not to remain in the boiling water.
- » We can choose instead to be proactive in our own health and wellness.
- » We can choose not to gain fat gradually by taking the necessary measures to prevent it to begin with.
- » We can choose not to make excuses like, 'that's part of life', 'it happens with age', 'my mother had diabetes

and was obese so I should follow suit' and 'the good life is too good'.

» We can choose to decide not to succumb to lifestyle-related diseases or excessive fat gain.

We can choose all the above and be the frog thrown into boiling water. We can also attempt to jump out. We can react in a timely manner. This choice, of course, has certain implications.

IT REQUIRES CONTINUOUS DISCIPLINE AND MINDFULNESS

One of the key ways of containing the gradual fat gain is a conscious and dedicated attention to diet and exercise. It is a lifelong journey, not something one does as a temporary experiment to get into certain clothes or be a certain size.

The type of diet one decides on is the integral part of the solution to the problem.

Diets that are rigid and exclusive of certain food groups are not sustainable as a lifelong choice for the most part. They may not be suitable for many. Starvation diets do not work in the long term. Foods that burn fat do not exist. You have to find your balance. You have to understand food, food groups and serving sizes, and experiment with eating until you understand your body's needs. You have to pay attention to how the body responds. You have to recognize signals of fullness, hunger, fatigue or over-exertion. You have to play an active role in what and how much you eat. This may mean cooking for yourself. It may require refusing certain foods at dinner parties. It may mean sticking with the plan the whole week irrespective of circumstances at work or home. It is not always easy, but once it becomes a lifestyle, it is so much a part of you that it is not an effort any more.

The type of exercise matters as well. Most women engage only in cardio-based exercises like running, walking, step or zumba. They believe this is the key to weight loss. They may add yoga a couple of days a week. Weight training, on the other hand, is not the norm for most Indian women. Building muscle is considered unfeminine. It so happens that **building muscle is the one thing that will keep fat gain in check**. Start early enough and build enough muscle mass and strength to take you through adulthood and old age with the minimum possible fat gain.

Weight loss is also analogous to the boiling frog. Lose weight rapidly (frog in boiling water) and you gain it right back (frog jumps out).

Lose weight gradually, one to three kilos a month, and like the slowly heated frog, your body begins to progressively get accustomed to its new environment. It registers the new eating patterns, the new exercise and other good habits. It absorbs these things slowly and makes it its own. After a year or two of such slow weight loss, regular exercise and clever, balanced eating, the body is unable to let go of its newfound way of life. Think of the frog in the slowly heated water. It cannot get out.

The culmination for the poor frog is different of course. We don't die from gradual weight loss; in fact, we survive and are better for it. The point I am trying to make here is the ability to adapt well, so well that you hardly recognize it. Once you taste the thrill of a healthier, fitter, slimmer, stronger life, it is hard to allow yourself to slide.

Recap

Our bodies acclimatize to the slow weight gain that happens gradually over the years. It is almost a certainty. However, we can prevent it if we react in a timely manner, like the frog thrown into boiling water. The only way to go about this is to:

- Start working out early in life.
- Eat sensibly as a lifestyle.
- Start training with weights as early and as regularly as possible.

2

FITNESS TRENDS

How to Choose the Right Programme for You

In a world of a multitude of choices for everything from the flavour of pasta sauce to face cream, it is only natural that we come up with a mind-numbing number of options for exercise as well. Whatever happened to good old walking and running? It seems to me a new exercise fad is born every week. Don't get me wrong. I think it is exciting. As someone who enjoys fitness and loves to experiment, it is wonderful to have so many options.

When I started out teaching fitness in 2000, there was basically only the stepper, floor aerobics, dancercise and jazzercise. Then came tae-bo and kick-boxing with fitness guru Billy Blanks and his high-energy routines. Aqua aerobics, zumba, bollyrobics and the numerous takeoffs on yoga have grown in the recent past to accommodate the ever-increasing need for variety. There are fitness trend forecasts by industry experts that predict which form of exercise is likely to be the most popular for the year. There are clothes and shoes made just for yoga and other specific exercises. It is a hugely profitable industry that is not necessarily only about fitness.

What does an average person do? How does she choose which kind of routine to follow? With advertisements that claim to get a person a flat stomach and slim waist by doing just cardio kick-boxing, it is easy to see how people can fall prey to such endeavours.

One should first understand one's basic requirement in order to build a strong foundation. The four pillars of fitness as given in my first book *Get Size Wise*) are:

Stamina, Strength, Flexibility and **Muscle Endurance.**

Once understood, you can decide what you want to do to improve each of these four pillars.

EXERCISES FOR STAMINA

Floor aerobics, walking, running, cycling, swimming, kick-boxing and zumba fall under the category of the first pillar of fitness.

Ask yourself what you enjoy the most. Use that as your staple workout. Do it twice or thrice a week. Fill in the other three days of the week with about thirty to forty minutes of walking or running. Use incline walking to strengthen muscles around the knees, which helps protect them.

EXERCISES FOR STRENGTH

Traditional weight training is focused on increasing strength and muscle mass. You have to start with traditional weight training with its usual lifts and curls to first and foremost develop a strong foundation. Building strong muscles around the knees and back will protect them from injury if you want to experiment with the latest fads in cardio.

Forms like boot camp, body pump, P30 X, cross-fit are strength-training sessions in varying formats which also kick up one's cardio to a very high intensity by the method in which the exercises are performed.

EXERCISES FOR FLEXIBILITY

Simple stretches and yoga work to fundamentally increase flexibility. Yoga also increases balance and core strength. Stretch every day. Even ten minutes of stretching is sufficient to keep you limber. If you enjoy yoga, sign up for a class two to three times a week.

EXERCISES FOR MUSCLE ENDURANCE

Improve endurance of muscles by adding to your routine low-intensity, long-duration exercises in the form of long walks, treks or cycle rides. These are mostly recreational.

WHY WEIGHT TRAINING SHOULD BE A PRIORITY?

Weight training increases size and strength of the muscles. This is particularly important for someone of Indian origin as we are inherently endowed with less muscle mass at birth (called sarcopenia).

Thereafter, having built that foundation of strength, experimenting with boot camp, body pump and other workouts is justifiable as by then, you have understood the nuances of strength training with external weights or with using one's own body weight. It is alright then to try out a cardio kick-boxing or zumba class. If you have established that strong foundation of strength, the chances of injury are minimized. When you attempt to attend a class where there are several students, with the trainer's attention diverted as she screams out instructions while trying to keep a watchful eye on everyone and working out herself, you will be able to take care of yourself. You will be mindful of how you perform each exercise, however difficult. You will recognize if something does not feel right for your body irrespective of what the trainer may say.

INJURY PREVENTION

Traditional weight training to build strength and muscle also helps prevent injury from other forms of cardio like step aerobics, zumba, Bollywood dancing, and other such exercises. Some of the moves encouraged in these classes are not always kind on the knees or hip joints. The incidence of injury went up drastically after step classes became popular, not because of the class itself but because students were not performing the moves following the necessary precautions, or had inherently weak muscles supporting the knees. Interestingly, Gin Miller, who originally brought out innovations to the Step Reebok, actually started doing the stepper to improve her knee strength following an injury. She obviously knew how to do it right and not injure herself further.

Similarly, the huge popularity of zumba has led to several back injuries as a result of all the hip shaking with weak cores and fragile backs. Women who rush to zumba classes may do so because it looks like a lot of fun. But they must first ask themselves if they are prepared for it.

If you inherently understand how to move correctly and have the necessary muscle strength and body intelligence to protect your joints with your muscles, then the chances of injury with these forms is minimal. If, however, you go in blindly with no clear understanding of body mechanics, you could twist a knee or injure the back trying those gyrations to mimic your instructor.

Some of these forms of exercise claim to include weight training or toning within their routine. They add 0.5-1 kg dumb-bells (honestly, even a baby's rattle weighs more than that surely?) which you are then supposed to move to music. Aside from the fact that this is a recipe for injury (yes, even with weights as light as 1 kg), one cannot build a respectable amount of muscle mass or strength with that kind of weight. I think these forms of exercises are a waste of time. You would much rather go through a traditional strength routine at a gym and use your jazzercise, stepper and floor aerobics as forms of cardio training.

STRENGTH TRAINING AND YOGA

Yoga improves flexibility. There is no question about it. Strength increments and building muscle from yoga is limited by the fact that the contractions are isometric and your own body weight is the ceiling. The way to circumvent that is to practise more and more challenging poses. Proponents of yoga would argue that it cannot be seen as just a form of exercise and is a whole lot more holistic than physical exertion, as it focuses on pranayams, kriyas and involves a lifestyle change.

Yoga, in my opinion, is a very important aspect of fitness. Those who train with weights will do well to include yoga and vice versa, contrary to the commonly held belief that those who do yoga should do nothing else. Especially not weight training. I think the two are complementary.

HERE'S WHY

Training with weights involves addressing one muscle group or a single muscle, strengthening it, increasing mass and improving its quality. I would think one of the great spin-offs of having stronger shoulders, chest, arms and core would be to be able to hold a challenging pose, like the Crane, for instance, during a yoga session.

Both forms of exercise focus on breathing. You really cannot train with weights or practise yoga without knowing how to breathe. Doing both brings home the concept and importance of breath.

Yoga greatly increases flexibility, which is beneficial in preventing injury while training with weights. At the same time, strengthening the various muscles of the body helps one perform yogic poses with better muscle control, preventing injury, and challenging and using those very muscles in different ways. Many Indian women I see practising yoga either force themselves into the poses or are not able to get into the poses required of them by exerting effective control over the muscles. Instead, they literally flop into the pose due to the sheer laxity of the joints or poor muscle tone.

Yoga helps you understand how to use your body as an entire unit and brings about a kinesthetic appreciation and sense of balance without the help of the mirrors in the gym. Weight training improves and creates even more body awareness as you focus your mind on individual or groups of muscles, watch yourself train, feel the burn and go beyond yourself to strengthen those muscles.

They complement each other very well indeed. Together they bring about a kind of balance of spirit between the calm introspection yoga demands and the deep, driven power weight training produces. Doing both, I think produces an endless loop of benefits that feed off each other. Love them both.

The wide variety of fitness forms to choose from is to accommodate this society of ours which suffers increasingly from Attention Deficit Hyperactivity Disorder (ADHD). We search for something different because we are easily bored. We want everything quickly so the latest fad that promises to be the easiest (and the craziest) way to quick weight loss naturally attracts us.

PRACTICE MAKES PERFECT

Here's the thing—practice makes perfect. You will have to concentrate on one thing long enough (ten thousand hours if you want to excel) if you want to do it well. When you are good at something, you enjoy it more. It is that simple. Flitting from one thing to another too often only sets the stage for injury and mediocrity.

It is good to cross-train and challenge your body in different ways. Not all of us can, though. (Refer to the chapter, What is your Fitness Personality? in my book *Get Size Wise*). Some prefer the simple act of running or walking for cardio while others enjoy music, dance and choreography. To each his own.

» Include the four pillars of fitness.
» Lay a strong foundation in strength and muscle mass.
» Learn to work with your required level of intensity in whichever form of cardio you choose. This means you need to know the routines and moves well enough to get your heart rate up to the required level.
» Choose your instructor or trainer wisely. The exercise form is only as good as your instructor or trainer is. A good instructor should know how to adjust the exercises and moves for your fitness level.
» Maintain perspective and a sense of humour. Fitness is supposed to be fun as well. Enjoy the journey!

Recap

There are innumerable options for fitness enthusiasts to accommodate our societies tendency to ADHD. In order to benefit from a fitness routine, you have to incorporate all the four pillars of fitness: *Stamina*, *Strength*, *Muscle Endurance* and *Flexibility*.

Stamina: If you are unfit or overweight, stay with walking or cycling for you cardio until you get fitter and lose some fat. Choose a class with a great instructor who understands your needs.

Strength: Only once you have built a strong foundation of strength with traditional weight training is it safe to experiment with other options. Ensure you have a good trainer initially; learn the exercises properly right at the start to prevent injury.

Muscle Endurance: Recreational sport, long low-intensity walks, treks, playing with the kids etc., fall in this category. **Flexibility**: Include stretching or yoga in your routine at least a couple of days a week.

If you are fit and strong, you can enjoy almost anything. Fitness then becomes fun and creative.

3

THE INDIAN PHENOTYPE

Too Much Fat, Too Little Muscle

We all know that people differ physically amongst cultures. Fat distribution, musculature, size, height, skin, eye and hair colour and facial features vary greatly. More and more evidence is emerging indicating that Indians suffer from what is called **sarcopenia** or low muscle mass. We are structurally smaller in build when compared to our Caucasian counterparts and in addition, we have less muscle mass and more fat for that frame. This clearly seems to put us at a disadvantage.

In a scientific study headed by Dr Scott Lear (from the Simon Fraser University in Vancouver, British Columbia, Canada) volunteers of European, Chinese, Aboriginal and South Asian descent were analysed. It was found that even among individuals with the same percentage of body fat, South Asians have a lower percentage of skeletal muscle or lean body mass. Asian women had less muscle mass than their counterparts of other ethnicities by at least two kilograms. The study also found that physical activity and exercise (both moderate and vigorous) was less among

Chinese and South Asians. In a follow-up study by the same author published in the *Journal of Clinical Endocrinology and Metabolism* showed that this body type with a higher fat percentage and a lower muscle mass is also more predisposed to diabetes.

The ongoing Nurse's Health Study, a very well-known and extensive study also shows that even for the same BMI, South Asian women seem to be at a higher risk for diabetes. The rationalization was the higher fat percentage and lower muscle mass.

Extensive research done in India by Dr Misra and his team has also revealed repeatedly that the typical Indian phenotype has a higher fat percentage and lower muscle mass, predisposing them to insulin resistance, diabetes, heart diseases and abdominal obesity.

Muscle is critical tissue. It is the metabolically active tissue in our body enabling us to be mobile. The lack of muscle could be the result of poor or improper nutrition (consisting of an abundance of carbohydrates and less protein) or a genetic trait.

Genetics and the environment may load the gun, but your lifestyle pulls the trigger.

Which brings me to touch upon the amazing field of epigenetics, which deals with our non-DNA inheritance. Habits and lifestyle can create change in our genes. So for instance, even if one is born with the gene for obesity, exercising regularly and eating well-balanced, healthy meals can change the way this gene expresses itself. In other words, this gene can get methylated or turned off. Genetics and environment, therefore, are inextricably linked.

While it may be true that belonging to Indian heritage predisposes one to having a lower muscle mass and a higher fat percentage, it does not necessarily have to play out that way if you don't want it to. Making the necessary changes in one's lifestyle goes a long way in changing the whole landscape of one's propensities and predisposition to obesity and other diseases. The earlier this lifestyle is indoctrinated into one's life, the easier it becomes.

The Indian diet is notoriously replete with carbohydrates. Make that the refined carbohydrates that we see today and the problem is compounded. Many Indians are vegetarian. This makes it even more likely that they eat a diet deficient in protein and inclusive of way too many carbohydrates. Most of us have no idea what our options for protein are (refer to the chapter on diet in *Get Size Wise*). This means we consume what pleases the palate, not necessarily what the body needs.

The urban Indian is also inclined to move little. With every gadget available to circumvent physical labour, an overdose of television, Internet and lazy living, it is easy to see why we have high fat percentages.

Most schools do not provide appropriately balanced meals. The young school-going girl is not taught to increase strength or muscle mass early on. Most of the physical activities revolve around cardio-based practices like running, cycling, swimming, and so on. Rarely do we see her doing push-ups, pull-ups, jumps, squats, lifts or any other form of muscle-building activity.

The young woman working in the corporate world leads a sedentary life and eats in hotels and canteens that are not exactly havens for healthy food. Living on her own, unwilling to cook, she orders in or eats out. This would not be such a problem if she understood what exactly she was supposed to eat and at least supplemented with salads, sources of proteins and worked out more.

She then gets married (she may manage to lose some weight just for the wedding, but then again that is mostly muscle since she, in all probability, dieted herself skinny to get into the wedding blouse). Life is hectic and a whirlwind of parties, socializing, working crazy hours, holidaying in exotic locations, eating randomly and exercising rarely. Once pregnant, she is encouraged to gain weight and is mostly pampered through her pregnancy. So she gains over 15 kg (of definitely not muscle), which she never loses between pregnancies.

It is an endless cycle of poor food choices, lack of the right kind of exercise (enough strength/weight training) and a sedentary lifestyle. It is no wonder then that we have low muscle mass and high fat percentage!

Most of the recommendations and advice on how to amend this state of affairs say include exercise with no clarity on what **kind of exercise**. This is mostly interpreted as aerobic exercise, so women start with walking and believe they have achieved their objective. The problem is, aerobic activity alone will not suffice in this case where the **primary concern is lack of muscle mass**. Doing cardio alone will not build muscles. In fact, focusing on cardio alone depletes muscle mass. Deliberately adding muscle by training with weights (yes dumb-bells, barbells, own body weight, machines etc.) is the only way to make a paradigm shift.

The rest of this book therefore, is on how to build muscle and related issues. This is not the easiest thing for the Indian woman to accept or absorb. We much prefer Bollywood dancing, low-intensity exercise, walking and yoga.

In the years I have been treating, counselling and training women, I have found that the average fat percentage is around 35 to 40 per cent before they start weight training seriously. I used the body-fat scale/calculator that utilizes bioelectrical impedence to evaluate body fat, water and muscle mass. Although not 100 per cent accurate, this fat percentage can be used as a reference point. Even apparently slim women of normal weight on the scale can have 28 to 32 per cent of fat. That is considered as the average fat percentage according to the American College of Exercise (ACE).

ACE Chart of Fat Percentage		
Description	Women	Men
Essential fat	10-13%	2-8%
Athletes	14-20%	6-13%
Fitness	21-24%	14-17%
Average	25-31%	18-24%
Obese	Above 32%	Above 25%

Due to their low muscle mass, even these slim women initially find it extremely difficult to perform exercises using their own body weight, like push-ups and squats. These exercises call for a certain amount of strength of the concerned muscles to be able to handle your own body weight. So even if you are heavy, you should ideally have enough muscle mass to be able to cope with that weight. Most women cannot. With adequate, serious weight training though, this can be reversed and even larger women should be able to handle their own body weight

I see things changing in some areas though. Many young women are taking to powerful forms of exercise, embracing strength. They are unafraid of bulking up as they are often cautioned (these are wildly propagated myths). I see a real thirst for knowledge. I see many women wanting to truly understand what fitness is about; to be fitter and stronger, not just to lose weight.

Recap

The Indian heritage ensures that we are, by and large, born with less muscle mass. This clearly puts us at a disadvantage, leaving us vulnerable to diseases like diabetes, high cholesterol and abdominal obesity.

The only way to circumvent this problem is to increase muscle mass by training with weights from an early age, eating enough protein and staying active through life.

4

CHANGE

Are You Ready for It?

You are probably reading this book because you are seeking change; a much-needed change in your body and lifestyle. You probably want to start exercising, lose weight, and get healthy. Or perhaps you are already exercising but not seeing the results you seek.

You should know that changes in the body are never isolated events. They have to be synonymous with changes in the mind. Without that flip of the mental switch, no change is enduring. Before going any further, try to recognize if you are ready for change.

ARE YOU READY FOR CHANGE?

You may desire it, wish it, will it, but are you truly ready for it?

There often is a turning point in one's life where one says, 'Alright! Enough with the poor eating habits, smoking, drinking and not exercising. I am going to change.'

This may come about as a result of a tragic event in

one's life, increasing discomfort in the body as a result of poor lifestyle that has finally caught up with you or a visit to a doctor's office. Or, you may just one day wake up with an epiphany.

It happens that it is not always easy. In fact it is most often not easy. Much as we all would like to introduce the right changes in our daily lives in order to improve our quality of life, and may even honestly try to, **change is never easy**.

I am quite sure a majority of the women I counsel and speak to during the course of my medical practice and fitness counselling already have a fair idea about the importance of exercise and healthy eating. Many have, in fact, already attempted different forms of exercises and experimented with different diets. Some are successful and many are not. They tend to vacillate back and forth between keeping up with a good routine and careful eating and completely letting go with no exercise whatsoever and a good deal of gastronomic indulgence.

Yet once you decide to make the change, the body inherently resists. A habit once formed (and laziness is a habit) is hard to break. The natural tendency is to find an excuse to not exercise.

There is an interesting theory called the *Transtheoritical Model of Change*, first elucidated by Prochaska and Goldstein in 1991. It says that change most often does not happen overnight in one swift transformation from one thing to another. A human being goes through several smaller changes before finally moving on, if at all. One can even apparently go through the preliminary stages and never really get off the Ferris wheel of change to take that final step. One can remain eternally circling through one of the earlier stages for months and years.

I have met several people who have been in one or the other of the preliminary stages of change for a long time. They will call me out of the blue to tell me they are going to start working out at the gym the very next day. They have questions.

What should they do? Could I inform my trainers? Could I send them a prescription for their exercise routine? How about their diet?

After a lengthy discussion and the promise to get back to me after their first workout, there is a peculiar silence for the next couple of months. The identical conversation repeats itself after six months.

Initially, I would have my secretary or trainers follow-up to check with them. Perhaps they lost their way to the fitness studio/aerobics class? Perhaps they fell ill? We would be met with several excuses such as sudden fatigue, unexpected travel or a visiting relative. Over the years I have learnt that no amount of reminders from our side really helps, unless the client truly wants to initiate the process of change.

I have had the same women meet me at every social function and tell me they want to start exercising. Perhaps seeing me acts as a trigger to remind them of what they are supposed to do. I honestly don't intend to impose or be any kind of reminder because I am fully aware that just meeting someone is not sufficient incentive for long-term change. They will even go to the length of asking specific details, phone numbers and so on. They may even take the next step and actually come in for a self-scheduled consult or a few sessions of exercise. However, they fail to follow through. Come the next social gathering and I can be rest assured of meeting the same women again with the same story.

I sometimes have no idea how to help. Then I realize that this is about their life journey and they can choose to live any way they see fit.

The following is a theoretical depiction of the various stages a person may go through before making necessary lifestyle changes. Some people (very few, I might add) seem to transition rather rapidly from wanting to make the change to actually changing (perhaps I have not witnessed the stages in-between.) The majority, however, seem to take a while to actually make the switch and most often, this switch is neither smooth nor easy.

THE TRANSTHEORITICAL MODEL OF CHANGE (PROCHASKA AND GOLDSTEIN, 1991)

One has to go through several stages to actually master altered behaviour. It may be of any kind (like de-addiction, alcoholism or cessation of smoking amongst others), but in this context, I am talking about starting a regular exercise routine and eating healthy to be fitter and lead a better-quality existence.

STAGES OF CHANGE

» Pre-contemplation
» Contemplation
» Preparation
» Action
» Maintenance
» Termination

PRE-CONTEMPLATION STAGE

Those in this stage have no intention of making any lifestyle changes (at least not for the next six months). They are typically in denial. They do not believe they need to make the change or that they might have a problem. Those around them, family, friends and their doctor, may advice healthier eating habits or exercise. To them, however, it seems pointless.

They may even go out of their way to avoid situations where they are subjected to lectures or where they are faced with their poor lifestyle choices.

People in this stage are difficult to treat.

> I have had husbands drag their reluctant wives to my office; women bring their unwilling (but perhaps curious) friends along for a fitness consultation. These people refuse to even consider that they may face some trouble as a direct result of their habits. Thus, they are in complete denial. I see the skepticism on their faces. The sidelong accusing glances at the culprit that brought them along to me. They are not in a place in their lives where they want to change.
> As a result, it doesn't happen.

I do not often see people in this stage as clients for a fitness consult. Those in this stage are mainly my patients in my medical practice. Women who have absolutely no intention of exercising and are suddenly told they need to. They are difficult to convince unless they have an immediate medical problem, like diabetes. In which case, the fear of complications of uncontrolled diabetes drives them to attempt exercise and diet.

Others tend to be highly resistant to counselling even if they are found to have high cholesterol levels or are overweight. There is no evident crisis, is there? So why the need for change? They usually blithely smile their way through the consult; promise to make changes and disappear, only to reappear months later with similar or worse complaints.

Those in this stage could also be women who are extremely thin/slim and believe exercise is not for them. I have spoken about the 'skinny-fat' person in my previous book. Suffice to say here that being thin/slim is really not a yardstick to measure health. Being fit is.

At the other end of the spectrum are women who are extremely overweight and perhaps have been for a large part of their lives. They may believe that it is futile to even try losing the weight. The task seems herculean and therefore, is not even attempted. For such women, the right kind of motivation and guidance helps. Deep down, somewhere in the recesses of their being, they want to change (unlike the skinny-fat ones), but believe they will never succeed.

Studies have shown that people most often regain the weight lost. So yes, it is not the easiest thing in the world. However, a consistent change in one's lifestyle has been shown to produce gradual improvement, however slow.

The key is to de-focus from weight and focus instead on fitness levels. Setting other goals not directly related to the scale, where one measures how fast one covers a certain distance or how much weight one can lift.

Learning a new skill that is movement-oriented, like attending a new class, are all ways to keep the exercise going without obsessing about the weight.

Continued exercise to improve fitness levels and better eating habits will eventually bring about weight loss and an improvement of health parameters like lowering of blood pressure and management of blood sugar.

CONTEMPLATION STAGE

In this stage, one is actually considering change. Perhaps a visit to one's doctor or an illness/death of a near and dear one has led to a reflection on one's own lifestyle. They may not be completely prepared or even equipped for the change but are actually contemplating it. In this stage, the individual usually discusses joining a fitness facility. They may even check out the costs, talk about the benefits and ask friends for advice.

PREPARATION STAGE

In this stage, the desire for change becomes more insistent. They try to seriously research their new, intended behaviour. They ask around. They make an appointment with a trainer perhaps. They may even try out a couple of classes or exercise sessions. They walk a few days a week. They may stop buying chips while grocery shopping. They may invest in running shoes and workout clothes. They may buy a juicer and filtered or cold-pressed oil.

The problem is, many people remain in this stage for

years on end. They are fully aware that they need to make the change in their behaviour but are simply unwilling to take the next step, which is making a commitment. They usually oscillate between being very interested in making the change and fleeing from it. They may at times be enthusiastic about discussing possibilities for change and at other times actively avoid people or situations associated with the same.

ACTION STAGE

Women in this stage are in the active process of change. They begin an exercise programme and start paying attention to food habits. They make the effort and actually do the work. But the chances of a relapse from this stage to any of the previous stages are also likely. **Action is only the beginning and does not necessarily forecast a successful end**.

MAINTENANCE STAGE

In this stage the woman persists with the behavioural change and action. She exercises regularly, stops smoking, eats healthy, and so on. She builds confidence. She starts associating more with like-minded people and makes serious attempts at changing food habits at home. She begins to try to incorporate fitness as a lifestyle. She may actually even begin to enjoy this newfound version of herself.

This stage of consistent change in behaviour should last for five years.

TERMINATION STAGE

When the maintenance phase has been sustained for a period of five years or more then the person is said to have established a habit. They exit from the cycle of change and the fear of relapse is minimal. The new habit becomes a natural part of their lifestyle.

If you want to change, you have to be willing to be uncomfortable (at least initially).

No one said change was easy, but most often, at least in this case, it is well worth the effort. The discomfort that comes with making the change is what often prevents most people from even trying. I am not just talking about the sheer discomfort of exercise itself, but everything that goes with it.

The adjustments that need to be made during the day in order to schedule the exercise hour.

- You may need to skip your favourite TV show or a session with your friends to accommodate your fitness routine.
- You may need to change your meal timings.
- You may need to get out of the house earlier to get to the gym before work.
- You may have to stay late a few days a week to fit in your routine after work.
- You may need to shop for different kinds of food to store at home.
- You may need to change your cooking style.
- You may need to sleep earlier than usual or wake up early.

All these changes cause discomfort. Discomfort to yourself and to your family. Being prepared (or at least aware) and anticipating the upheaval can help cushion the ride to some extent.

One must fully understand that at any stage during the course of the various stages of change, one may relapse. There is every chance of it. An illness may set you back. Travel and holidays often derail your good intentions. Once you have reached higher up in the stages of change, the Maintenance and Termination stages for instance, there is every possibility that even after a relapse, you will get back on the saddle ready to keep going.

The stages of change are not written in stone, however. I do know women who make the switch from a completely unhealthy lifestyle to a more conscious one suddenly and quite literally overnight. There are not many such women, but I have met some and have the greatest admiration for them.

FACTORS INFLUENCING CHANGE

Society, friends, family, career and most importantly, one's own sense of self-worth plays an important role in the ability to introduce change.

» If one has support on the home front with people to look after the kids or help with the cooking arrangements, of course it is easier to take an hour or two for yourself to exercise.

» If your workplace supports wellness, has a well-equipped gym with the necessary guidance to exercise provided, then it becomes easier to get in a workout before or after work.

» If you work close to home or even from home, it is definitely easier from a time perspective.

On the other hand,

» If your commute to work takes hours and you are completely fatigued just by the travel, then exercise before or after is a superhuman task.

» If you have no family support, or anyone to take care of kids, old parents or the cooking, taking time away from home is next to impossible, especially if you are a working mother.

The social setting of your life therefore plays a critical role in you being able to lead a healthier life. Poorer segments of society do not have the means to buy healthier, better-quality food. Neither do they exercise. In all probability, they work to make ends meet and eat what they get. It is cheaper to buy fast food on the street than fruits and vegetables. The choices, therefore, are obvious and limited for someone who is economically challenged.

Ankita came from a very wealthy family. She began working out with Training For Life (TFL) programme in her teens and loved it. When she was in her early twenties her parents arranged for her to marry a very rich man who lived with his extended family in another town. He owned a huge business and that seemed to thrill Ankita as she excitedly told me of her future plans to take care of the business.

When I met her several years later, she had become

extremely overweight, depressed and was a different woman. Her life hadn't panned out the way she had expected it to. Living in semi-rural India in a joint family meant she had to cook and look after the men folk practically all day long, leaving her no time for herself.

Exercise?

That was out of the question. She said she sometimes tried to exercise in her room early in the morning before everyone else woke up.

As for looking after the business?

That turned out to be a fantasy too, as everything was already well taken care of by the men in the family. I think Ankita was in shock for the most part of the first few years of her marriage. I could only commiserate with her when she spoke about it.

She went back and forth with trying various things to improve her life.

After having her two children, she was determined to do something to change her life. She said she had to. Else it would destroy her.

A few years later she called me one day to tell me she had started her own business with her husband. She went to work every day, exercised despite the obstacles and sounded so much happier that I could only be excited for her.

I know it could not have been easy. She had waited almost eight years to achieve what she wanted. Even something as simple as exercising had met with so much resistance.

There are many women I meet who are in a similar situation, often restrained by family and society. Some manage to make that shift from continuing to please people and neglecting themselves, to moving beyond that. Some do it very well. Some falter and slip back into old ways which are so much more familiar, even if unbearable. Some make drastic life decisions to move on permanently for their own peace of mind.

Whichever way you look at it, change is not easy.

For those who are not hindered by external or internal issues, the decision to make time for exercise depends on other things like the ones I have already elucidated. Working your way around your own unique set of problems will take some effort and adjustment, not only from you, but also from your family members.

There may be some amount of social programming that influences change. For instance, in most conservative communities, exercising, going to a gym, training with weights, even wearing workout clothes is frowned upon. It then becomes more difficult for a young woman to break free from this setting. I have come across several young girls, married into conservative families where the mother-in-law does not approve of her leaving the house to go work out. Where is the need for it? She had enough work to do in the house taking care of everyone else. Or, following delivery, women are strongly discouraged from exercising. It is almost a taboo. This kind of indoctrination makes it difficult to change.

Change is not easy. It does not happen overnight. It usually (but not always) happens in stages. If one truly desires change for the better in terms of weight loss, decrease in disease risk and so on, it may be necessary for you to make some difficult choices in order to sustain these changes. Until that point, however, things will not change. The final decision to make the change is like a light bulb coming on inside the brain, an epiphany or an 'Aha' moment if you may. You decide that it's time for change and you are willing to do all it takes to make a difference.

Recap

In all probability those reading this book are seeking change. In this case a better-quality life, better health, weight loss, and more. Even perhaps a change in the understanding of fitness and health.

This requires a paradigm shift in thinking before making any actual change in behaviour. It then requires the incorporation of lifestyle changes. Change does not happen overnight. It usually goes through the several stages until the final stage of termination is reached.

Chances of one relapsing back to original lifestyle habits are high and need to be kept in mind.

There are several factors that influence the ability to change, including our family, friends, home and work environment and social setting. We can, however, work around our own set of issues to achieve successful change.

5

MAKING CHOICES

We Are Defined by the Choices We Make

Contrary to what we may like to believe, most of us do have the luxury of choice. Choices, of course, have consequences. As I have already said in the previous chapter, some choices are not easy and may edge you out of your comfort zone. The consequence of the choice, however, has to be viewed from a larger perspective.

» You could choose not to exercise regularly and set yourself up for various lifestyle diseases like obesity, diabetes and hypertension.

» You could choose not to train with weights and build muscle and thereby lose about a pound of muscle and gain two pounds of fat every year.

» You could choose to eat unhealthy, fried, oily food from your office canteen or you could choose to take a healthy packed lunch from home.

» You could choose to walk more and sit less.

» You could choose to give up your TV programmes and go for a run while listening to music instead.

» You could either choose to make time for exercise or choose to spend that time watching television, surfing the Internet or socializing.
» You could choose not to stock unhealthy snacks or buy them and then be tempted to eat them.

These are all choices with consequences.

AGAINST ALL ODDS

» I know several mothers who prefer to bring their kids to the exercise class.
» Women who choose to play with their kids as a form of work out.
» Women who work out to a DVD while the child sleeps at home.
» Women who get their husbands to baby sit while they work out.
» There are women who plan ahead for their meals several days in advance.
» Women who shop over the weekend to ensure they are well stocked with enough vegetables, fruits and proteins.
» Women who make little Ziploc bags of snacks of nuts and seeds to carry with them while travelling or to take them through long work days.
» Women who cook and store for several days.
» Women who plan ahead while eating out and choose restaurants that also serve healthy options.
» Women who snack at home before heading out to a party.

Then there are women who have such a well-trained staff at home that the household is like a well-oiled machine. The maid knows about the smoothie that needs to be served in the morning. She remembers to pack healthy snacks for the kids. She has the delicious salad ready when evening rolls around and working people come home hungry. There is fresh fruit on the table, soup on the stove and a wonderful roast in the oven.

So, it all depends on one's life situation. **It is about making the right choices**.

When clients narrate their home scenario and use it as a reason for not being able to find the time, I may begin by making suggestions for possible change. Very often, however, most suggestions are immediately shot down as impossible. There always seems to be a reason why it cannot be done or poses to be far too difficult.

So here's the thing—you have to first choose your priority. Decide if it is important enough to cause some amount of discomfort for yourself and your family, at least initially. If you think it is, then you will have to stop saying it is impossible and make it possible. No one except you can make it possible, and if you want it badly enough, you, and only you, can make that choice.

CHILDHOOD EXPERIENCES

The whole process of making the right choices and attempting change is also influenced largely by childhood experiences.

A child who has been exposed to a healthy lifestyle, parents who are conscious about the food eaten at home and regular exercise themselves, children exposed to games and physical activity as a natural part of childhood will find it that much easier to get back to thinking along those lines. The brain has already understood and perhaps even enjoyed that lifestyle and physical activity. Getting back to it then is not quite as alien as for someone who has essentially been sedentary all her life.

The process of making the choice to change her lifestyle as an adult is far more difficult for someone who:

- Has never been very active as a child.
- Has wiggled her way out of every gym class in school.
- Was perhaps overweight as a child.
- Used food as a solution to everything, from sadness or joy to celebration or reward.
- Has parents who have never exercised or been active.
- Has been exposed to eating out indiscriminately or ordering in with no concern about the quality or quantity of food consumed.

Those women who have been athletes or played sports in school would also find it easier to train their bodies to be physically active later on. They have what is called Muscle Memory of what it is to be physically active.

Childhood athletes don't automatically become fit adults however. As I have seen after a survey I took of hundred middle- and upper-class women, many women who were athletes in school completely neglect their fitness, wellness and weight with age. On the contrary, some women who were never active in school wind up being very fitness conscious.

The children of sedentary, unhealthy parents grow up under these influences. It becomes so much a part of the hard wiring of their brain that it is their natural state of living. There is a whole generation of such parents and young children. For them, making the switch will be a much harder task. Be conscious, therefore, of what you expose your kids to.

There are repercussions to such a lifestyle:

» A higher incidence of diseases likes diabetes and hypertension at a much younger age.
» More and more women are seen to be afflicted by coronary heart disease at a much younger age.
» An epidemic of depression and other mood disorders has set in.
» Young women, with a lot of money to spend, but an appalling lifestyle.
» Young women who burnout in their careers because they are unable to handle the stress and unhealthy existence.

There are other factors that may influence the choices you make. Sometimes we tend to get emotionally secure in our comfort zone, however physically uncomfortable it may be. Starting to exercise regularly involves many things besides just getting yourself up early to get to the gym or out for a run. There may be resistance or emotional blackmail at home. There may be antagonism from friends or co-workers. Change is never easy for anyone. If it is important to you, however, you have to make the effort even against resistance.

Interestingly, it is the pregnant women who appear to be the most receptive to incorporating change in their lives. Perhaps the fact that they are now hosting another life makes them feel more responsible and receptive to it. This seems to be a great time to influence lifestyle modification, including introduction of regular exercise, which is what we attempt to do with the ante-natal patients at my hospital. Although pregnancy is not the best time to begin an exercise programme, it is an opportunity to positively influence women with the hope that they will continue healthy lifestyle habits well past their labour and delivery.

MAKING THE RIGHT CHOICES

Do it for yourself: Wanting to change for someone else mostly fails. You are the only one constant in your own life; others come and go and are certainly not responsible for your choices. Very often, women start a fitness routine in order to impress a significant other or because they have been told to. With the right motivation, and if they stick with it long enough, hopefully somewhere along the way they discover that they are really doing this for themselves and begin to appreciate it. Repeatedly remind yourself why you have made this choice. Sometimes it is hard to remember all the benefits of exercise when you are actually going through it.

Is it worth it? You ask yourself as you sweat through a routine. Remind yourself of how good you feel after the workout, of the long-term benefits, how good you are going to look and more importantly, how much better you will be emotionally.

Make a commitment: Making a commitment to yourself is perhaps the first step to making a change. Unless you are sure you want to change, there is every chance you will find a zillion excuses to discontinue. The commitment could be in the form of a 'Note to Oneself', a reminder posted on your mirror, a reminder on your phone and so on.

Assign a mentor: Having a mentor, perhaps someone who has journeyed along a similar path of weight loss, could be an important source of inspiration. It could be a friend, sibling or even your instructor or trainer. Having a connection with someone who understands what you are going through can encourage and guide you, and keep you motivated.

Join a supportive community, or recruit a friend to be your cheerleader: A support group, like friends from your gym or group class could be a very important part of being successful in making the switch from your old lifestyle. It is hard to do it alone. Sometimes, your family may not be in it with you. I have counselled many women who struggle with managing their menus and meals, which are completely inconsistent with that of the rest of the family. Women sometimes have little support at home. In these cases, the one thing that keeps them afloat is a support group outside of home. If you have a supportive family set-up, consider yourself lucky.

The journey through the process of change is sometimes a lonely one. You have to adjust to changing paradigms and sometimes uncomfortable situations where the old patterns do not suit your new lifestyle.

I have women tell me they have had to fall out with old friends from their past life because their changing behaviour did not fit in with that friendship. (They could not go drinking and binge eating for instance) It is a choice you have to make. If your well-being is important to others, they will understand and appreciate your changing behaviour. If it is not, then you will have some difficult decisions ahead of you.

Set goals with the help of a professional: Goal-setting is an art and science. Your goals have to be achievable while challenging you at the same time. Setting a goal to lose 5 kg in a week is setting yourself up for failure. If you do succeed, you can be sure the success is short-lived.

Once you decide on making a change for a better lifestyle, set short-term and long-term goals. Set several small goals related to the various aspects of your fitness; your flexibility, your strength, your diet and your stamina. That way you are ensured of succeeding in at least 50 to 60 per cent of the goals you set, which in itself is a motivating factor.

Self-monitoring: It is important to monitor progress at regular intervals. Once a fortnight is a fair amount of time for a quick reassessment of progress. Without self-monitoring, it is easy to drift along with no clear purpose and no visible progress.

Ask for feedback and get reinforcement: Get regular feedback from a professional. You may find you are doing better than you believed. Or, you may find there is a better way of doing something.

Create incentives: All human beings need incentive. Create your own incentives for success. A new dress after losing the first 5 kg for instance. A massage after the next 3 kg. These incentives keeps the body happy and appreciated.

Food does not have to be the reward or incentive. In fact, using food as reward is perhaps what got you here in the first place. Eating food should be a joyful experience when the body requires it. Small quantities of a variety of foods to your satisfaction can be continued right through any fitness programme so one does not develop cravings and feelings of deprivation.

Good, tasty food, in the right quantities, should be a part of your programme, not a reward for reaching your goal.

Prepare for setbacks: Occasionally, injury, unexpected work commitment or travel could set you back. Be prepared for these setbacks. Have a plan. Keeping a 'holiday workout' ready, for instance, will ensure you do something through your holidays. Planning ahead of eating out with guests or for festivals would mean you prepare to be a bit different from others around you. Alternatively, you could choose to ease off during these times and allow yourself some indulgences with a clear plan to get back on the wagon as soon as possible. There is no point beating yourself up and going into a tailspin after.

Boosting your belief in yourself: Positive self-talk and believing in yourself is probably the most important aspect of successful changed behaviour. It is terribly easy to drown in negativity, especially when things do not go as smoothly as you think they should. It may so happen that you are unable to comply with diet restrictions for a couple of days. Or, you may need to miss your workout occasionally.

Feeling defeated by a few setbacks and giving up at the first signs of difficulty is a sure way to take two steps forward and three steps back. This could well be a pattern for some.

Pick yourself up and move on!

The difference between those who manage to stay on track despite obstacles in their way is purely their belief in themselves that they can!

Making appropriate choices can be life-changing. Only *you* are responsible for the choices you make. Therefore, let them be the right ones.

Recap

Most of us have the luxury of choice. We just have to be ready to face the consequences.

Making the right choice for yourself can be made possible by:

- Doing it for yourself
- Reminding yourself why you made this choice
- Making a commitment to yourself
- Assigning a mentor to help you through
- Joining a support group
- Self-monitoring
- Asking for feedback
- Creating incentives
- Preparing for setbacks
- Boosting your belief in yourself

6

SET-POINT THEORY

Why It Is Difficult to Lose Weight and How to Overcome This?

Weight loss and gain does not happen overnight. It takes time for the body to gain or lose weight and acclimatize to the new weight. As seen in the story of the boiling frog, the body takes time to adjust to a new environment. When the change in environment is slow, the body adapts to the new environment (the weight) better.

The *Set-Point Theory* states that our body tends to sustain a certain weight over a long period of time. This is almost like a weight thermostat that maintains a steady weight over time. This means that even when you try to lose weight by doing a lot of cardio and by dieting, though the body may lose weight initially, it will tend to try and go back to its original weight by creating hunger, and making you eat more or exercise less. It is almost as if the body is trying to hold on to its excess weight. This is because the body recognizes that original weight as its set-point and tries to maintain it.

It is the same with weight gain. One or two days of feasting or overeating will not cause you to gain weight. The body readjusts after a few days and you remain at your original weight. It is after days and months of overeating (and lack of exercise) that weight gain occurs. Similarly, it is after days, months and years of under-eating (and exercising) that you lose weight. In both cases the body tends to try and sustain the original weight.

This original weight the body recognizes as 'normal' is the *set-point* for that body.

The Set-Point Theory (which has been refuted but is a basic theory about energy balance) states that the body has a tendency to find a certain 'set-point' of weight. This maintenance of weight is through several pathways in the body.

» Signals of hunger and satiety through the release of hormones like leptin and ghrelin.
» Through the stabilization of blood sugar by insulin.
» Through neural pathways from the hypothalamus in the brain.

Clearly, our hormonal milieu changes with age. For women, the physical changes they go through in their life cycle are to a large extent responsible for their weight changes.

» *Menarche:* The onset of the physical maturity and the menstrual cycle during the teenage years.
» *Pregnancy:* With its onslaught of hormones and weight gain to support another life.
» *Breastfeeding* (for about a year): Which essentially burns a large number of calories and if managed properly by eating right, can help you lose the pregnancy weight.

» *Menopause:* The dropping estrogen levels, perhaps the onset of hypothyroidism, can lead to a change in the way the body handles calories and energy.

These hormonal cycles, however, are not responsible for huge oscillations in weight. They can be controlled and managed effectively with the right exercise routine and food habits. The enormous amount of weight gained by most women over the years is due to large energy excess. Increased and improper (too many refined carbs, unhealthy fats and processed food) food intake and decreased expenditure.

Tanya had gone through several cycles of weight loss followed by weight gain before she came to meet with me. She was frustrated and discouraged by the oscillating weight. She wanted a permanent solution and was willing to work hard and long for it, she said.

'It's not about working out for long periods of time and starving yourself.' I tried to explain to her. 'It's about working smarter, more intensely, adding weight training and eating better.'

She was used to doing one-and-a-half hours of cardio every single day (without a day off) and starving herself half to death most of the time. Every time she took a break, went on holiday for instance, the weight would be back, with interest. This was partly because she tended to binge eat on holiday and did absolutely nothing physical. But it was mainly because she hadn't changed her 'set-point', so her body wanted to go back to what it believed to be the 'correct weight'.

The solution was to change her set-point.

I started her on serious weight training. After the initial resistance, she got quite excited about the weights. She couldn't believe she was doing only twenty to thirty minutes of cardio every day.

'Are you sure that's enough?' She would ask me.

She also could not believe she could eat as much as she did! This was almost twice as much as she was used to on her usual 'diet'.

After six months of serious training, she looked like a different woman, firmer, toned and leaner. She went off to Italy on a holiday for three weeks. She came back looking as fit as before.

She had indulged, she said. 'Who wouldn't in Italy?' But, she had also walked a lot.

Her body had changed its set-point to a lower value. It had gained muscle mass and altered its metabolism. She could afford to take a few days off from exercising and indulge once in a while without worrying about regaining lost weight.

Let's say you gain weight by overeating and lack of physical activity to gradually reach a weight of about 80 kg. After several months of this weight, the body recognizes this weight as the new set-point. It then begins to balance energy intake and expenditure to sustain this weight.

Once exercise and calorie restriction begins, there will be an initial resistance by the body in the form of hunger in order to maintain the body's original weight. On continuing the calorie restriction and exercise, however, the body begins to go into an energy deficit and taps into fat stores leading to fat loss. After the initial few kilos of fat loss, the body tries to find a new set-point and hovers around that weight, balancing calories and energy. Often, however, the body tries to revert to the original set-point by creating hunger and increasing the intake of energy. This could be one of the reasons why it has been found that dieters tend to regain lost weight. This is why it is so difficult to sustain the lost weight.

HOW DOES ONE BREAK THROUGH THIS 'SET-POINT'? SET A NEW ONE AND LOSE MORE WEIGHT?

We need to change our Set-Point. To do this, we need to actually change the very working of our body, not just lose weight.

Our body has what is called a Basal Metabolic Rate or BMR. This is the basic calorie requirement that is necessary for the day-to-day functioning of the body. Digestion, respiration, cardiac activity and movement through the day requires calories and is sustained by our BMR. Some people have a higher BMR than others. They require more calories just to sustain basic day-to-day activities. If we can raise our BMR it is possible to lose fat. With a moderate amount of calorie restriction and exercise we would go into a calorie deficit and start to lose fat.

» If daily calorie intake (or food you eat) is equal to the BMR plus calories burnt during exercise, then your weight is maintained.

» If daily calorie intake (or food you eat) is less than BMR plus calories burnt during exercise, then you will lose weight.

Therefore, to lose weight you can:

» Consume less or
» Increase BMR to increase calories burnt during exercise and at rest.

There is a limit to which you can lower your calorie intake. Extremely low-calorie diets are not sustainable, as we have repeatedly seen in research. The dieters tend to go back to eating their original calories and gaining back the weight. The more sensible thing to do would be to lower the calories slightly (to a manageable level, where you do not feel extreme hunger) and increase BMR and calories burnt through exercise.

Calories burnt through exercise is easy to understand. You exercise more. But obviously there is a ceiling to that as well. You can't exercise endlessly. Increasing BMR, on the other hand, will help burn more calories.

HOW DO WE INCREASE OUR BMR?

By building more muscle. The key to a highly metabolically active body, with a higher BMR is building muscle with weight training.

The human body is a miraculous piece of equipment. It is truly amazing. I am awed every time I operate on a patient and see the various organs so carefully organized, functioning perfectly, for the most part.

If we want to make changes to it after abusing it for years and creating obesity (with its associated problems), we need to be respectful of the fact that the body has struggled to stay functional even in the overweight state and has done everything in its power to maintain a near-normal day-to-day existence for you. Reversing the process cannot be achieved overnight, much less with unfavourable methods like starvation diets, extreme exercise or weight-loss drugs. It has to be approached scientifically and gradually.

Recap

Ways to lose weight and sustain it and set a new 'set-point':

- By far the most important method of changing one's set-point to a new level and be able to maintain it at a new low is to **train with weights to increase muscle mass.** Muscle is a metabolically active tissue and acts to increase our BMR. The more muscle you carry, the more calories you burn, even at rest.

- **Lose weight gradually** and allow the body time to **acclimatize** to new set-points (the gradually heated frog) before attempting to lose more. Weight plateaus, therefore, need to be respected and tided over with patience and continuing to exercise. This is clearly the reason why rapid weight loss eventually leads to regaining the lost weight and sometimes putting on even more.

- **Avoid extreme low-calorie diets**. The body lowers its BMR to accommodate this low-energy intake. Starvation diets and fad diets do more harm than good in the long term. The body senses this low- energy intake and interprets it as famine, lowering its energy expenditure to save it. Going too low on calorie intake is eventually counter-productive as it not only harms the finely tuned hormonal orchestra within the body, but it also leads to subsequent binge eating and weight gain. This is the opposite of what you want to achieve.

- **Avoid yo-yo dieting and weight-loss cycles**. Several cycles of gaining and losing weight leads to a dysfunctional metabolism. It wrecks havoc in the internal workings of the body, like the release of hunger and satiety hormones, stress hormones and insulin. The body is, therefore, unable to stabilize at a healthy weight as it struggles to accommodate ever-changing energy intake and expenditure.
- **Besides exercise, try to be physically active** throughout the day. The calorific expenditure of daily physical activity cannot be underestimated. Although it is not classified as 'exercise', moving around through the day will keep the calories burning.

7

WEIGHT, SIZE AND FITNESS

Keeping the Perspective

In my previous book, *Get Size Wise*, I had discussed the weighing scale, its significance and irrelevance. Suffice to say here that the scale is an overall measure of what one weighs inclusive of muscle, fat, bones, brain, and other parts of the anatomy. It is an easy and simple way to keep the general perspective. It is, however, not the only or the best way to assess fitness. Neither is your size. Being a certain size (however small) is not a representation of your fitness level.

WEIGHT AND SIZE ARE ALWAYS THE PRIMARY FOCUS FOR WOMEN

Two women weighing the same may appear visually very different. This is the result of the composition of their body. Are they carrying more muscle or fat? A more muscular body with less fat appears leaner, shapelier and more toned. As you exercise and gain muscle your weight on the scale may remain the same or may even increase slightly. If the measurement of your waist decreases, clothes fit better and if you are getting stronger and fitter, then you are progressing in the right direction irrespective of the scale. Most women who start exercising in earnest eventually learn to de-focus from the scale.

I have watched this happen with joy and gratification amongst my own clients. Regular, serious exercisers are rarely consumed with the numbers on the scale. With time, they start valuing their body for what it can and cannot do rather than focus on what it weighs. They are more mindful of the signals like hunger, thirst, boredom, fatigue, muscle soreness, improper exercise form that the body sends, rather than being preoccupied with admiration and comments from others.

For them, being able to work out regularly, decrease their timing on their run or walk, being able to lift heavier weights with better form, being able to hold the Downward Dog or Plank positions in a beautiful, perfectly comfortable manner is more important.

THE WAISTLINE

Probably, the one size that really matters from a health perspective is the size of your waist. Fat accumulation particularly within the abdominal cavity is catastrophic for the heart. Keeping a close watch on your waist circumference is a good way to keep a check on what's going on within you. A widening waistline is indicative of fat accumulation in the wrong place. Abdominal fat is also slightly different from the fat that lies just under the skin in, let us say, the thighs. Abdominal fat is metabolically active fat that releases toxic hormones that are detrimental to the health of the heart. It is not only the aesthetic that is skewed with a widening waistline but the all-important working of the heart.

For the Indian population the cut-off values for waist circumference have been reduced to correlate with the higher risks posed for Indians, and are:

- Men – 90 cm
- Women – 80 cm

Where do you measure the waist?

Just above the level of the iliac crest or the bony edge you feel at the lower end of the waist on the side. This corresponds usually to the level of the navel or slightly below.

Keeping a log of a decreasing waistline is a very clear indicator of fat loss as opposed to muscle loss.

We are all born with a different frame. Some may have a wider bony frame, while some are slight with narrow shoulders, hips and an overall smaller structure. Everyone has a unique distribution of muscle mass. Some have more muscle on their legs, with very poor muscle in their upper body, while others have the reverse. We can correct this to a large extent through weight training to build muscle in the weak areas. Each of us also tends to be genetically prone to accumulate fat in particular areas of the body. Similarly, losing fat occurs the way we are genetically programmed to lose it. While one woman may lose the fat first from her hips and thighs leaving the abdominal fat for the end, another may lose it first on her upper body and abdomen, leaving her thighs and hips for the end.

There is no such thing as spot reduction. You exercise, eat clean and you start to lose fat (perhaps, a bit slower than the initial fat loss, nevertheless) in areas you are programmed to. Eventually, if you persist long enough, if you train diligently and watch that calorie intake, you will lose those last few kilos.

> The weighing-scale obsession has transferred to the younger generation in a frightening way that could only spell enormous vulnerability for their future health. Young girls routinely starve themselves to stay slim. They only exercise if they feel they need to lose weight, not as a routine, and rarely to feel good. Their perception of what they have to look like is so skewed that it borders on the ridiculous. I have had young girls tell me they don't drink alcohol at parties but have no reservations accepting uppers in the form of tablets, or do drugs because it spares them the calories!

SHAPING YOUR BODY

The body is already beautifully shaped. Every muscle has a specific contour. The size of the muscles may differ between individuals. This shape of the muscle, however, is most often camouflaged under several layers of fat so what we see in not truly the shape of the underlying muscle but the layers of fat that are layered over the muscle. In order to see the shape of the muscle, **the fatty layer has to be minimized. Correspondingly, the fat percentage of the body has to drop.** For this to happen, we need to continue to work towards a slightly negative calorie balance with exercise and balanced eating. As we continue to train and lose the subcutaneous fat and build the muscle underneath, the actual shape of the body emerges.

Here is an interesting phenomenon:
It is almost impossible to build very large muscle mass (as in the fear of bulking up most women have) unless you are eating a large excess of calories, especially protein. The body can only do one thing at a time:

- Lose fat while on a calorie deficit and/or training, or
- Build muscle (if you are training with weights) while on an adequate calorie intake or
- Add fat if you are on a calorie-excess regime and not training.

If you are trying to build large volumes of muscle, you have to eat more and train more. This is what bodybuilders do. If you are trying to lose fat and at best, trying to build *some* muscle or at least maintain your current muscle mass, you will have to eat at an adequate or at a slight calorie deficit but not go too low on intake. Simultaneously, you have to train with weights to maintain that muscle mass. This is one of the reasons why starving yourself does not work when the objective is to build muscle and lose fat.

Eventually, once you have burnt most of the fat you need to and are at a reasonable fat percentage, continuing to train with weights (with some cardio) and eating at a higher-calorie intake will help build more muscle mass. If that is what you want.

If, however, you are doing only cardio and not

building any muscle, you will have to continue to do a *lot* of cardio and eat a *lot* less just to stay in the same place.

You have to decide which route to choose in order to stay in shape.

- Enough food with weights plus some cardio
  or
- A lot less food and lots of cardio

MUSCULAR DISPARITY OR IMBALANCE

During the course of a fitness assessment, it may be noted that certain muscles in the body are deficient or weak while others may be stronger or larger. Ideally, the opposing or antagonistic muscles, which have opposing actions in the body, need to be balanced for a properly functioning and fit-looking body. The physiology of muscle imbalance is discussed in the chapter on muscles. Here, the aesthetic are explored.

For instance, the quadriceps, a group of muscles at the front of the leg, are the largest muscles in the body. The hamstrings, a group of muscles at the back of the leg, are much smaller. The quads extend the knee joints while walking or running and the hamstrings flex the knee-opposing actions.

Often, we find an extreme disparity between these two groups of opposing muscles in terms of strength and size. They are inherently different in size, but there should be a balance between the two. When the quads are much larger, as is seen with many runners, those attempting only step class or using only the stepper in the gymnasium could end up with not only back pain or bad posture, but also odd-looking legs!

» Tight chest muscles (the pecs) and overly stretched and weak back muscles, lats, rhomboids and trapezius will lead to a hunched posture with shoulders rolled forward.

» Flabby abdominal muscles cause the abdomen to protrude even if there is very little fat over or under the muscle, giving the impression of a wide waistline and potbelly.

» Poor back strength not only causes bad posture but also causes the pelvis to tilt forward and the abdomen to stick out.

» Inadequate glute muscles, which is a very common occurrence especially with age, leads to a flat-looking butt. Training the glutes helps tone and shape these muscles.

» Undertrained arms will lead to flabby arms that jiggle with every movement, particularly the portion over the tricep muscle.

» Overtraining certain parts of the body while neglecting others could also result in aesthetic and functional problems. Many men particularly, are in the habit of training their upper body excessively while neglecting the lower. They end up with huge arms, chest and back supported by spindly legs — aesthetically and functionally peculiar.

All the above are muscular problems that can be addressed with the right weight-training exercises. Doing specific exercises will not burn fat in that particular area but it will improve the muscle. There is no such thing as spot reduction of fat. But, yes, you can 'spot improve' your muscle.

GAINING FAT

Here is the truth, however. As we grow older, most of us do have to contend with some fat accumulation in areas where we may not want it. The right exercise and diet will control fat gain to a large extent but most of us have to accept a change in the shape of the body with age. Exercise can be used to maintain fitness, increase confidence about our bodies and definitely control and contain weight gain. I am not sure if trying to reclaim the body we had as teenagers is healthy, or even wise.

USING THE SCALE WISELY

Initially, it may be important to see the scale move (and it will, in fact, quite rapidly if you are doing it right). With time and regular exercise, especially with weight training, you start building muscle, which weighs more than fat and the scales may seem to stall a bit. This is the time to de-focus from the scale and focus more on getting fitter. After a certain point of regular exercise and healthy balanced eating, you stop wanting to jump on the scale. You really do. It seems irrelevant. You are more focused on the way your clothes fit and the way you feel rather than the numbers on the scale. Getting fitter through exercise is more satisfying than just getting thinner or lighter. The discipline that comes with a regular exercise programme in addition to thoughtful eating is the reward in itself.

Recap

- The weight reflected on the scale is not a true indication of fitness or the quality of your body.
- The measure of the waistline is a true indicator of fat loss.
- There is no such thing as spot reduction. You cannot lose fat in one area alone.
- You can, however, build muscle in that area alone and strengthen and shape it if required.
- Weight training is the only thing that can address issues like muscle imbalance or weakness.
- The scale needs to be kept in perspective.

8

HORMONES AND FAT LOSS

The Internal Orchestra Influencing Fat Loss

There are several hormones that have been investigated extensively with regard to fat loss. The internal orchestra, the hormones, also controls how much we eat, how we respond to the food we eat, how we store fat and how we build muscles. Some of us are adept at losing fat and/or building muscle. Genetics and our hormonal milieu play a prominent role in these abilities. This does not mean we leave everything to 'destiny' and allow ourselves to grow to enormous proportions without intervening just because of hormonal setbacks.

The irony is that disturbances in the hormonal balance are often set right with the right amount of exercise and diet.

Exercise seems to be the treatment and the cure for:

» Insulin resistance
» Leptin resistance
» Metabolic syndrome
» Hunger
» Satiety

» Poor growth-hormones secretion
» Too much stress-hormones secretion

In this chapter, I will discuss some of the important hormones responsible for fat metabolism:

» Insulin
» Leptin
» Human Growth Hormone
» Ghrelin
» Thyroid Hormones
» Catecholamines and endorphins

INSULIN

This hormone has received a lot of attention recently. It is well known that insulin is the anabolic hormone. The primary effects of insulin on carbohydrates, muscle and adipose tissue are:

Carbohydrate Metabolism

- Insulin increases the rate of glucose transport across the cell membrane.
- It increases the rate of glycolysis (or breakdown of glycogen) by increasing hexokinase and 6-phosphofructokinase activity.
- It stimulates the rate of glycogen synthesis and decreases the rate of glycogen breakdown.

Lipid (fat) Metabolism

- Insulin decreases the rate of beakdown of fatty acids or lipolysis in adipose tissue and hence lowers the level of fatty acids in the plasma.

- It stimulates fatty acid and triacylglycerol synthesis and storage in the fat cells.
- It increases the uptake of triglycerides from the blood into adipose tissue and muscle.
- It decreases the rate of fatty-acid oxidation in the muscles and liver.

Protein Metabolism

- Insulin increases the rate of transport of some amino acids (essential for muscle growth) into muscle tissues.
- It increases the rate of protein synthesis in the muscles, liver and other tissues.
- It decreases the rate of protein degradation in muscles (and perhaps other tissues).

These effects of insulin serve to encourage the synthesis of carbohydrates, fat and protein; therefore, insulin can be considered to be an anabolic hormone. This means that once we consume food, the insulin levels rise, preventing the metabolism (release or utilization) of stored fat and promotes the breakdown of available glucose instead. This known action of insulin is the reason many (particularly the proponents of low-/no-carbohydrate diets) theorize that fat loss is much easier if the carbohydrates are reduced, irrespective of the consumption of proteins and fats. They claim that insulin prevents the release and metabolism of fatty acids (which it does when glucose is available as a substrate for energy). This, however, is solely a post-prandial (post-meal) event.

According to researcher Dr John Ivy, University of Texas, the hormone prevents protein breakdown and also boosts protein synthesis within muscles, in addition to preventing the breakdown of fatty acids. This is the reason the hormone is called an anabolic hormone. The role of insulin, as we all know, is to keep blood sugar on an even keel. In order to do this, insulin promotes the use of the available glycogen in the blood. It also prevents the use of fatty acids. The only time this happens, however, is immediately after a meal.

Through the day, the utilization of stored fat will depend entirely on the total number of calories (energy) consumed and not just the release of insulin after a particular meal. Naturally, if the total energy consumed is more than energy expended, the stored fat will not be utilized and will remain as stored fat. If the energy consumed is less (whether from carbohydrates, protein or fats) then the body taps into the fat stores. Singling out carbohydrates and insulin as the root cause of obesity can be misleading. It is the combination of excess calories (from various sources) and a sedentary lifestyle that ultimately leads to excess storage of fat. Insulin, in fact, has been found to decrease one's appetite, not increase it.

The argument then, is how do people with insulin resistance, who have high levels of circulating insulin, gain fat?

Metabolic Syndrome

In the condition called insulin resistance and metabolic syndrome, the problem occurs when cells in the body do not respond to insulin. The levels of insulin may be high but the cells are insensitive to the instructions given by the hormone. The levels of circulating insulin, therefore, are greatly increased in an attempt to try to reach the cells, ineffectively. These levels are raised alongside other symptoms of metabolic syndrome like higher cholesterol levels, widening waistline and pigmentation of the skin.

This is a syndrome of symptoms which causes obesity. Which came first—the obesity, expanded waistline, the high cholesterol or the higher insulin levels in response to the insulin resistance and glucose intolerance—is a good question.

The solution is regular exercise. What is required is regular aerobic activity to burn enough energy and weight training to increase the basal metabolic rate of the body.

A diet with lower carbohydrates and a higher protein intake has been found to help with weight loss, as already mentioned.

How does a high-protein diet cause weight loss?

Westerterp-Plantega (along with colleagues Sofie Lemmens and Klaas Westerterp) reviewed high-protein diets. In their review paper, they wrote that controlled trials show that the reason for weight loss with higher-protein diets (1.2–2 g/kg/day as opposed to the normal 0.8 g/kg/day) like Atkins, South Beach Diet, Paleo, etc., is not the relatively lower-carbohydrate content of the diet but the higher-protein intake.

The increased dietary protein acts in three different ways:

» Increases satiety.
» Stimulates energy expenditure.
» Spares fat-free muscle (helping to maintain resting energy expenditure or BMR).

Westerterp-Plantenga's hypotheses are now supported

further by another study of which she was the lead author. The study compared two energy-restricted diets, one normal in protein (0.8 g/kg/day) and one higher in protein (1.2 g/kg/day) on seventy-two overweight and obese men and women. While both groups lost weight, as expected, the group that consumed more protein retained more muscle and had a higher resting metabolism (this was independent of physical activity).

LEPTIN

Leptin arises from the Greek word *leptos*, which means thin. Leptin is the satiety hormone. In other words, it signals satiety when the amount of fat stores reaches a certain level. Leptin, therefore, is the long-term satiety hormone. Though released by fat cells, it reaches the brain where it has receptors in the arcuate nucleus near the hypothalamus. By attaching to these receptors, it sends signals to other parts of the body to stop eating.

Leptin Resistance

Seeing that it is released from fat cells, circulating leptin levels are higher in obese people with more fat cells. However, instead of curbing hunger in the obese, it was found that they have a certain level of leptin resistance similar to insulin resistance. They are unable to react or respond to the signals sent by leptin and continue to accumulate calories and fat.

» It has been proposed that consistently eating a diet rich in fructose and processed carbohydrates (especially from a very young age) can deregulate the leptin system and lead to leptin resistance. The body becomes insensitive to the signals sent out to and from the brain to control energy intake.

» Dieters who lose weight experience a drop in levels of circulating leptin. This drop causes a decrease in the BMR and other reversible changes are seen in thyroid activity, sympathetic tone and energy expenditure of skeletal muscle. The result is that a person who has lost weight has a lower BMR than an individual with the same weight who has never lost weight. This is a known fact and one of the reasons why weight loss through diet alone is not the best way to achieve sustained weight loss.

» All these changes are mediated by leptin. They are the homeostatic responses meant to reduce energy expenditure and promote weight regain. (Back to a 'set-point' the body tries to maintain). A continued, slightly lower-calorie intake along with exercise will reset the homeostasis and the leptin level and leptin sensitivity return to normal.

Role of Leptin

- Leptin is the satiety hormone.
- It is secreted from the fat cells and acts on long-term satiety and energy balance.
- When fat stores are adequate, leptin signals satiety.
- It also signals the thyroid releasing hormone (TRH) to stimulate thyroid stimulating hormone and the other thyroid hormones like T3 and T4.
- The receptors for the satiety signals of leptin are found in the hypothalamus of the brain (besides other areas in the body for its other functions)

> very close to the receptors for ghrelin, the hunger hormone. The brain, therefore, is the primary controller of hunger and satiety.
> - Individuals losing weight through diet alone have a lowered BMR initiated by leptin as a way of conserving energy.
> - There may be a defect in the leptin sensitivity in some people with obesity causing them not to recognize satiety. This leptin resistance can be treated with continued regular exercise and a lower-calorie intake with adequate proteins.

Leptin has various other functions besides satiety, some of which are yet to be defined.

HUMAN GROWTH HORMONE (HGH)

The human growth hormone is produced in the brain by the pituitary gland. It is critical for growth and development in children. Tissue repair, brain function, metabolism and energy are also important functions of the HGH throughout our lifespan. This hormone has been found to reach its peak in the teenage years, when there is the growth spurt, after which it declines gradually. A number of physiological stimuli can initiate HGH secretion, the most powerful, non-pharmacological ones being sleep and exercise.

Sleep

HGH is released in a pulsatile fashion that follows our circadian rhythm. Getting to bed at a decent hour and getting about six-eight hours of uninterrupted sleep is important for the proper release and functioning of HGH.

Exercise

The exercise-induced growth hormone response (EIGR) is well recognized and although the exact mechanisms remain elusive, a number of reasons have been implicated.

Cardio or aerobic exercise

EIGR is closely associated with the intensity, duration, frequency and mode of endurance exercise. A number of studies have suggested that an intensity threshold exists for EIGR. Exercise intensity above the lactate threshold and for a minimum of ten minutes appears to elicit the greatest stimulus to the secretion of HGH. Exercise training above the lactate threshold may amplify the pulsatile release of HGH at rest, increasing 24-hour HGH secretion.

In other words High-Intensity Interval Training or HIIT works very well to increase EIGR.

Resistance training

Weight training or training against resistance has been found to produce the maximum EIGR. This is particularly true while lifting heavy weights with adequate rest between sets. The actual growth of the muscle tissue with protein synthesis is aided by an insulin-like growth factor.

Growth hormone as an anti-ageing hormone

The growth hormone has been touted as an anti-ageing hormone due to its physiological effect of increasing lean body mass and decreasing fat percentage in the body. Ageing is normally associated with an increase in fat percentage and naturally declining HGH. It is also often associated with a progressive decrease in the volume and, especially, the intensity of exercise.

A growing body of evidence suggests that higher-intensity exercise is effective in eliciting not only beneficial health, well-being and training outcomes but also in greatly improving body composition. In many cases, the impact of some of the deleterious effects of ageing could be reduced if exercise focused on promoting the EIGR.

Athletes have sometimes abused this ergogenic effect of HGH. They take it in the injectable form to improve their performance and muscle mass. The adverse effects, however, are far greater than benefits. The hormone is not FDA-approved for use, either for anti-ageing purpose or improved athletic performance.

Role of the HGH

- Growth itself.
- Fat metabolism.
- Maintenance of a healthy fat percentage, muscle mass and body composition in later life.
- Exercise, especially HIIT and resistance/weight training elevates EIGR and is a significant and well-recognized method of elevating HGH naturally in the body.
- Responsible for the remodelling and turnover of muscle tissue, bone and collagen.

GHRELIN

This is the hunger hormone. The cells in the gastrointestinal tract and stomach release ghrelin in response to hunger. It is secreted when the stomach is empty. When the stomach is stretched or full, the secretion of the hormone stops. Ghrelin is the short-term switch, signalling satiety, acting immediately after the intake of food. During a fasting spell, ghrelin conserves glucose metabolism, directing the body to utilize fat stores instead. It also creates the hunger response to fasting, leading to food-seeking behaviour.

Ghrelin acts by combining with receptors in the brain to signal hunger. The receptors for ghrelin are in the same brain cells as those for leptin. Both these hormones are therefore, very closely related in controlling energy consumption and maintaining weight.

Role of Ghrelin

- Ghrelin is the hunger hormone.
- It counters energy deficit by enhancing hunger.
- During fasting, it aids in conserving carbohydrates and promoting fatty-acid oxidation.
- In the post-prandial state, it contributes to satiety.
- It favours energy storage and glucose oxidation.

New research suggests a range of new roles for ghrelin, including addictive behaviours, cardiovascular protection, neuroprotection and regeneration and perhaps the ageing process.

THYROID HORMONES

Thyroid hormones also have a role to play in weight maintenance. They are primarily responsible for maintaining metabolism. Those who suffer from hypothyroidism (where the secretion of the hormones T3 and T4 are below normal) have a tendency to gain fat. This deficiency can be corrected very easily with the thyroid pills and on taking them correctly, the deficiency is rectified and the weight is regulated.

Role of Thyroid Hormones

- To increase the BMR and the heat production of the cells of the body.
- *Lipid Metabolism:* Thyroid hormones stimulate fat metabolism, mobilization and fatty acid oxidation.
- *Carbohydrate Metabolism:* Thyroid hormones affect carbohydrate metabolism and work in concert with insulin, enabling entry of glucose into the cells.
- *Growth:* Thyroid hormones are necessary for normal growth in children. The effect of these hormones is closely linked with growth hormone.
- Maternal hypothyroidism in pregnancy can lead to problems such as mental retardation in the baby. These hormones are important for brain development of the foetus.
- The hormones are necessary for normal blood flow to the various organs by affecting the cardiac output and contractility of the heart muscle. The decreased blood flow to the peripheral tissues seen in hypothyroidism is the reason for the cold intolerance noticed in these patients.
- Normal levels of the thyroid hormone is necessary for the normal functioning of the neural tissue. Hypothyroidism can lead to mental sluggishness and depression while hyperthyroidism can lead to anxiety or nervousness.
- The thyroid hormones are essential for the proper functioning of the reproductive physiology. Infertility and poor pregnancy outcome can result from abnormal thyroid states.

Hypothyrodism has been found to be more common among women than men, particularly around the pre-menopausal period. It is worthwhile, therefore, to do a thyroid screening for women over the age of forty.

Hypothyroidism is often used as the reason for weight gain. I have many clients/patients who claim they cannot lose weight because they are hypothyroid.

Point is, if they are being treated properly and they are euthroid (normal thyroid levels after medication), their metabolism should get back to normal and with the right exercise routine and diet, they should be able to lose weight over time. Blaming a disease (which has been corrected) cannot help deal with the problem which is being overweight. It seems to me that some women sometimes prefer to play the blame game and are unwilling to change their behaviour and lifestyle to change their bodies.

A case in point was a conversation that went something like this:

After a book reading of mine, a woman in the audience stood up and asked —

She: 'I have hypothyroidism doctor, so I can't lose weight'.

Me: 'Haven't you been treated?'

She: 'My doctors have tried to diagnose me. They say it's very difficult to treat. I have hypothyroidism so I can't lose weight'.

Me: 'Are you on medication for the hypothyroidism?'

She: 'Yes.'

Me: 'So essentially, if you are taking the medication,

your thyroid hormones will be normal. So you should be able to lose weight with the right exercise and diet.'
She: 'But I can't. My doctor told me I have hypothyroidism and that is why I am overweight.'
Me: 'Well, what can I say?'

CATECHOLAMINES (EPINEPHRINE AND NOR-EPINEPHRINE) AND ENDORPHINS

Catecholamines, epinephrine and nor-epinephrine are produced in the adrenal glands situated on top of the kidneys. Catecholamines are released in situations of stress where a fight-or-flight response is required. They are also known as the stress hormones.

How then does the release of stress hormones during exercise lead to better stress management?

Stress hormones are released temporarily during an exercise session, after which the levels return to normal. Stress hormones are so said to be depleted with bouts of intense exercise, leaving the body with less of the hormones and a better response to stressful events through the rest of the day. Trained athletes are found to have an even greater response to exercise, leading to a higher release of the catecholamines.

While working out, another set of hormones called endorphins are also released. These are the feel-good neurotransmitters from the brain, spinal cord and many other parts of the body, which create a feeling of euphoria and well-being. They consequently reduce levels of stress.

HIIT has been found to produce significant elevation in the levels of catecholamines (epinephrine or adrenalin and nor-epinephrine), cortisol and HGH (Boutcher et al, 2011). The catecholamines drive the release of fat, especially abdominal and visceral fat, from fat stores so it can be burned by working muscles.

Role of Catecholamines

- The release of catecholamines during HIIT leads to post-exercise appetite suppression.
- Reduction of body-fat percentage, especially abdominal fat, is more after a session of HIIT than low-intensity long-duration cardio. Catecholamines, along with HGH, appear to be responsible for this fat oxidation.

Clearly, several hormones (besides a number of other mechanisms working in concert within the body) are responsible for fat loss and muscle gain. There has been extensive research done to try to elucidate the best methods to gain muscle and lose fat. Eventually, however, we know it is the total energy balance at the end of the day/week that will ascertain fat loss or gain. Eating a higher-protein/low-fat/low-carbohydrate diet that is still high in calories and failing to exercise to expend those very calories will eventually lead to weight gain.

Recap

- There are several hormones that are implicated in the metabolism of fat—insulin, leptin, human growth hormone, ghrelin, thyroid hormones and catecholamines and endorphines.

- Each of them play a unique role in storing or utilizing the fat (besides other nutrients) in the body.

9

MUSCLE

Your Most Prized Possession

WHAT IS A MUSCLE?

Muscle is the soft tissue that lies beneath the fatty layer and skin in the body. It covers the bones, surrounds the joints, pads the body and is responsible for movement. Without muscles attached to the bones and the joints, the body simply cannot move.

TYPES OF MUSCLE

There are different kinds of muscles:

Smooth Muscle: The smooth muscle or involuntary muscle as it is called, is found within the walls of such organs as the intestines, esophagus, lung bronchi, uterus, bladder, blood vessels etc. Unlike skeletal muscle, smooth muscle is not under conscious or voluntary control.

Skeletal Muscle: The skeletal muscle is found on our skeleton, attached to the bones by means of the tendons.

These muscles are under our voluntary control through signals from the brain. The skeletal muscles are responsible for movement. These are essentially the muscles we train when we participate in resistance training exercises.

Cardiac Muscle: The cardiac muscle is, as the name implies, the muscle of the heart. It appears similar in structure (striated) to the skeletal muscle but it is an involuntary muscle.

TRAINING THE MUSCLE

When we talk about resistance/weight training or the second pillar of fitness, we are referring to the skeletal muscles. The cardiac muscle can also be trained when we challenge the cardiovascular system with any kind of exercise that raises the heart rate. Even a resistance-training or weight-training routine done without rest and at high intensity, can train the cardiac/heart muscle, much like cardiovascular exercises.

In order to strengthen and grow the skeletal muscle, it has to be challenged. This means that it needs to work against more external force than it is normally accustomed to.

Given our current social setting, most women don't do much physical work that challenges the muscles. Initially, for most women, even training with weights as light as 2 kg could be considered a challenge. Of course, it goes without saying that one needs to eventually move on, beyond that threshold, to start lifting heavier weights in order to grow the muscle.

Training the muscle against resistance is done using dumb-bells, kettlebells, barbells, one's own body weight or weight machines. The choice is a personal one.

» Free weights or dumb-bells give us a greater range of motion.
» Weight machines are restricted in their mobility and range of motion. They are also usually designed keeping specific exercisers in mind. Machines made in the US for instance, may be made to accommodate much taller people, making it difficult for the smaller-built Indians to use.
» One's own body weight is used in exercises like push-ups and squats. They rely on the challenge produced by lifting one's own body weight.

It makes sense to use all these options to get the best out of all the systems.

HOW DO MUSCLES ACT TO CAUSE MOVEMENT?

Muscles are attached to the bones by means of rope-like processes called tendons. Bones are connected with each other at the bony joints like the shoulders, hips and knees by means of ligaments. Movement usually takes place around these joints. Two bones (or sets of bones) are brought together or apart around the joint leading to movement. The contraction and relaxation of the muscles around and attached to a joint causes the joint to move.

For instance, when we walk, the hip flexor muscles of the hips and thighs contract to flex or bend the thigh towards the torso. Simultaneously the knee joint is also brought into play, flexing the knee by the contractions of the hamstring muscle in the back of the thigh. While this happens in one leg, the other leg extends at the hip and knee joint with the aid of the gluteal muscles of the butt and the quadriceps at the front of the thigh. Running is similar to walking except that the movement is so swift that even before one foot strikes the ground the other has already been lifted. So at some points we are literally airborne while running and it is the power generated from our muscles that creates enough momentum for this to play out.

We do not really think about it. It just happens from *muscle memory*. We do not have to tell ourselves, 'now bend the knees of the front leg', or 'extend the thigh backward by contracting the glutes'. It happens almost automatically as a result of instructions from the brain through the nervous system, stimulating the various muscles.

MUSCLE ATROPHY

We learn to walk at an early age, usually by the age of one. As children (if we are lucky), we move a lot, running, walking, climbing, falling, jumping, carrying things, digging, lifting, kicking, twisting and a whole host of other movement patterns that engages the musculoskeletal system in different dynamic ways.

These days, not all kids enjoy this luxury of movement. They are mostly seated either in a classroom setting, and that too in badly designed chairs, or in front of a television or computer. Movement seems to be restricted to the absolute minimum.

As we age, most women tend to move less. I am talking about movement on a daily basis, not scheduled exercise. We tend to sit, stand or lie down a lot. The muscles, therefore, are not called upon to do anything that challenges them.

I have seen young women sauntering out of the supermarket, usually chatting on the phone, with a man Friday in tow carrying their groceries. Is it really too much of an effort to even carry our own groceries? It may also seem that attempting such mundane day-to-day activities is a waste of time and effort.

However, this time and effort is well spent, triggering the neurons in our brain to signal the muscles of our limbs to work. When this happens, our muscles recognize that they are essential for the human body and are required to function so they continue to do so. On the other hand, muscles that are never called upon to work or do anything strenuous decide their role in the body is not terribly vital and the neurons from the brain firing instructions to these muscles die a slow death until it seems as if one is practically paralysed.

In essence, unless the musculoskeletal system and the central nervous system are continuously called upon to actually function, they forget to do so.

Not so with the involuntary muscles of our respiratory, digestive, cardiovascular genitourinary or immune systems. These continue to work and function even when we do not necessarily or consciously work them. Rarely do we need to remember to breathe or digest our food after a heavy meal. It just happens.

The musculoskeletal and central nervous systems are closely interconnected (as is every other system in the body with the central nervous system). With continued disuse of the muscles, the neurons required for the functioning of these very muscles degenerate, just as the muscles themselves degenerate and atrophy. They shrink and shrivel. They stop functioning effectively.

Movement, balance, strength, flexibility and reflexes are affected. Increased incidence of falls, loss of balance, back pain and knee pain is the result of lack of strength and functionality in the relevant muscles. A single history of a fall with injury sets you back even further and the enforced bed rest will cause additional atrophy of the muscles. It is a vicious cycle.

The only way to break this cycle is to train the muscles to start doing what they were supposed to do in the first place: move, work against resistance, lift, contract, expand, push, pull, hold you up, and so on. Building enough muscle mass will eventually reverse the atrophy.

Meena was fifty-three years old when she developed knee pain. After five years of massages, traditional medicines and physiotherapy, I finally met her. I told her she needed to start weight training to increase the muscle mass and strength around the knee joint. I tried to explain that weight training was the only way she would recover from her 'weak knees' as she put it. She was not impressed.

'Muscle training?' She said. 'I don't like that.'

'Well, it's not exactly called "muscle training" but, I suppose it could be. Point is, that's your only hope. Why don't you like it? Have you tried it?'

'No, but I have heard about it. You lift all kinds of things to bulk up.'

'You have been misinformed. Weight training can be tailored to your requirement. In your case, you will only do exercises to strengthen your knee joint. Not to "bulk up" as you say.'

That appeased her somewhat. She started with some basic exercises to strengthen the quads, glutes and hamstrings. She did a lot of stretches to relieve the tightness in the hamstrings and hip flexors. After the first two weeks and just six sessions, she felt enormously different.

She could walk without wincing. She could stand up without holding on to the sides of the chair.

'Maybe I should continue this "muscle training" for the rest of my body,' she slipped in one day while reviewing her protocol with me. I pretended, of course, that it was a completely normal request, given her initial aversion for this 'muscle training' and proceeded to formulate a total body routine for her.

Today, she is in love with her 'muscle training' as she calls it. She trains seriously four times a week. She feels stronger, safer and is so much more confident.

MUSCLE IMBALANCE

Most muscles in the body appear as pairs. We have a pair of bicep muscles at the front of both upper arms, a pair of tricep muscles at the backs of both upper arms, a pair of rectus abdominis muscles running from the rib cage to the pubic bone forming part of the abdominal wall, a pair of soleus muscles or calves, and so on. Ideally, as with any engineered structure, both sides need to be developed perfectly in size and strength for balance.

Most muscles also have antagonistic pairs of muscles on the opposing side of the body. By this I mean, muscles with opposite actions. The bicep and triceps muscles, for instance, are antagonistic muscles lying at the front and back of the arms respectively. The bicep muscles in both the arms flex the elbow joint, bringing the hand up to the shoulder, while the triceps muscles do the reverse and extend the elbows. These antagonistic pairs also need to be balanced in shape and size, not just for aesthetics but also for proper functionality and stability.

Have you ever seen a circus tent?

In order for a circus tent to stand up tall and straight, and look aesthetically beautiful, well balanced, the central pole, the supporting poles and the guy ropes need to be stable, equalized and of a certain resistance. If one is tighter than another on the opposite side of the tent, the entire structure is likely to appear skewed. Not to mention that it is likely to collapse.

Similarly, in our bodies, if the muscles on one side are tighter or stronger than the ones on the opposing side, the body is likely to be imbalanced. This muscle imbalance will eventually culminate not only in bad posture, but also pain and injury.

Weight training is particularly useful to correct muscle imbalance. If the hamstring muscles at the back of the thigh are much stronger than the quadriceps muscles at the front (as it often is for many people), the result is back pain and a penchant for injury. Weight training can specifically train the hamstring muscles to increase in strength and size to balance the quads. Similar problems could arise if the abdominal muscles are weak, placing all the strain of holding the body upright on the back (opposing) muscles. The result is back pain and a slouching posture.

There's nothing worse than poor posture. Being as slim as a waif or curvaceous would be of no importance if your posture is not correct. Posture is one of the primary aspects of the body that has to be focused on when beginning a weight-training programme.

MUSCLE HYPERTROPHY

Muscle hypertrophy is the scientific term for the increase in size of the muscle fibres. The number of fibres in each bundle of muscle remains the same. With training against resistance, these fibres increase in size. They also develop micro tears during training process, which heal to form stronger bonds of fibrous tissue, making the entire muscle bundle stronger.

The minor tears caused by the training process lead to what we refer to as Delayed Onset Muscle Soreness or DOMS. DOMS arises about twenty-four hours following a training session. It usually subsides within forty-eight hours.

The amount of hypertrophy or increase in size of the muscle is primarily genetically determined. It is also controlled largely by testosterone, the male hormone. High levels of testosterone enable hypertrophy of muscle fairly easily with training. Women, however, inherently have lower levels of the hormones and genetically less muscle mass. Growth of muscle even with training is much slower and never really to the same extent as in men.

The objective of weight training is hypertrophy or muscle growth. It is of great benefit to women to increase their muscle mass. Not only will it make them stronger and shapelier, but will also increase their BMR. This increase created by the increased muscle will ensure more energy consumption and less fat accumulation. This is particularly so with age. The ageing process otherwise lowers the BMR, leading to fat accumulation and a change in body composition even if you continue to eat the same amount of food and do only cardio.

Individual muscles and groups of muscles can be trained with weight training. That is the uniqueness of training with weights. We can address specific muscle imbalances, strengthen specific muscles and change the alignment of the body. Women who train with weights are able to carry themselves better than those who don't, simply because they build stronger, more balanced muscles with the right training routine.

FLEXIBILITY IN MUSCLES

It is pertinent to mention here that stretching the very same muscles is also very important in maintaining balance. After training them against resistance using dumb-bells, barbells, one's own body weight, kettlebells, or whatever you might have at your disposal, they need to be stretched. Flexibility is the fourth pillar of fitness and plays an important role in maintaining muscle health. Overly tight muscles arise as a result of lack of flexibility. Healthy muscles are strong and flexible. Lack of flexibility not only leads to muscle imbalance and poor posture, but also makes one more prone to injury.

The objective of an exercise programme should be to make your body more efficient at burning calories, keeping you burning fat and ensuring that you stay lean for as long as possible. This objective can only be achieved by building muscle.

Recap

- The muscle is your most priced possession.
- There are different kinds of muscles in our body and the ones we train during weight-training sessions are the skeletal muscles.
- Without adequate training, muscles undergo atrophy and can become imbalanced.
- Increasing muscle will increase BMR and the ability of the body to burn fat and stay lean.
- Weight training, therefore, is of prime importance if you want to retain a strong, shapely, functional body.

10

FAT

The Fat in Your Diet, the Fat in Your Body

THE FAT IN YOUR DIET

All edible fat is not evil and complete paranoia towards this food component is somehow unwarranted. In fact, consumption of healthy fats such as the monounsaturated and polyunsaturated fats has been found to reduce the incidence of heart disease. It is also required for various essential functions of the body including healthy-looking skin and hair.

Fat adds flavour to the food. Fat-free food tastes dreadful. This is the probable reason why it is often loaded with salt, sugar and other additives to make it palatable. This makes us eat more of this fat-free food, seemingly guilt-free, when in reality, we end up consuming a huge number of calories, not all of them necessarily healthy or nutritious. This is a marketing trick. You would much rather eat a little of the real thing with some healthy fats in it and exercise regularly rather than concern yourself with the fat-free circus. Fats induce satiety and a sense of satisfaction. Foods with even small quantities of fat create more satiety and gratification than something with no fat at all. It allows us to eat less and feeling more satisfied than eating huge volumes of fat-free junk and feel quite incapacitated at the end of it.

According to the American Heart Association, in your daily diet about 25 to 30 per cent of your total calorie intake can be from fats. Of this 30 per cent, it is advised that only about 10 per cent come from saturated fats. For instance, a woman consuming a 2,000-calorie diet can get 600 calories or approximately 66 grams of fat per day, where every gram of fat provides 9 calories.

For those who have heart disease, have had cardiac surgery or have high cholesterol levels in the blood, keeping the saturated fats to the absolute minimum is advisable. A restriction of 20 per cent of calories from fat is advised.

SATURATED FATS

Saturated fats are present mainly in meats, poultry, eggs and whole-fat milk products like ghee and butter. Certain vegetable oils like coconut and palm oil also contain saturated fats. These saturated fats need not be avoided altogether, however. Small quantities of good-quality ghee and butter, eggs, even red meats are safe and good for health.

Coconut oil and other coconut products have been vilified extensively in the past but the presence of the medium-chain fatty acids found in coconut is now found to have some health benefits. It is even touted as a cure-all for several ailments including obesity, heart disease and cancer, though this has never been clearly proven by genuine research. Pure coconut oil contains no hydrogenated fat and has 92 per cent saturated fat, the highest amount of saturated fat found in any fat. Coconut oil, like most other oils, is a mixture of various fatty acids. It is a blend of 44 per cent lauric acid and approximately 16 per cent myristic acid, a unique combination which has been found to have certain health benefits.

Before you go running out to the store to buy yourself a bottle of coconut oil to drink, however, remember that although coconut oil has no cholesterol (unlike animal fat or milk products) it still has saturated fat and needs to be used with caution, especially for those with a history of heart disease.

HYDROGENATED FATS OR TRANS FATS

Hydrogenation of fats is the process of adding hydrogen to the fats primarily to increase their shelf life. Such fats are used in baked goods that are packaged and are meant to be long-lasting. This process leads to several health problems on consumption, such as the raising of Low Density Lipoprotein (LDL) cholesterol and heart disease.

Some animal fats and whole-milk products also naturally contain small quantities of trans fats. A majority of hydrogenated fats are manmade, however.

Far worse than eating saturated fats is consuming packaged and processed food products. Think twice before buying packaged products, whether baked or fried. Indulgences like chips or cookies need to be few and far between. You would much rather eat a cake baked with love at home with real cream and butter once than buy packaged cupcakes that claim to be low cholesterol or high in vitality.

Heating oil to a very high temperature, cooling it and then reheating it also leads to the formation of trans fats. This is seen most often in restaurants or in street food where the same oil is reused and reheated several times. When deep frying (occasionally) at home, use small quantities of oil that can either be used completely or the remains discarded.

MUFA AND PUFA

Monounsaturated and polyunsaturated fatty acids, MUFA and PUFA, are found mainly in fish, vegetables, nuts and seeds. These fats are a healthier option for consumption when compared to saturated fats.

Saturated Fats or Trans Fats	Polyunsaturated Fats	Monounsaturated Fats
Butter	Corn oil	Almond oil
Lard	Fatty fish like salmon, mackerel, sardines	Walnut oil
Meats, especially beef and pork	Soybean oil	Olive oil
Poultry, especially the skin	Sunflower oil	Peanut oil
Coconut oil	Sesame oil	Avocado oil

Palm oil, palm kernel oil	Brazil nuts, walnuts, peanuts, pine nuts, pecans, almonds	
Partially hydrogenated oils	Flax seeds, sesame seeds	Sunflower seeds, pumpkin seeds
Full-fat dairy products		
Egg yolks		

Choose your fats wisely. Use a combination of oils for your cooking at home. Try and source cold-pressed or filtered organic oils rather than refined oils. The refining process also leeches the nutrients from the oil.

Fat once consumed can either be used for energy, especially if there is a paucity of carbohydrates or glycogen (which is the primary source of energy), or it can be stored in the fat cells (see Chapter 11, 'A Day in The Life of Fluffy').

Excess consumption of carbohydrates or proteins can also be converted and stored as fat in the fat cells. Fat, therefore, is excess energy that is stored for a famine. Here's where the problem arises. Most often, that day never comes around. We have enough and more food all year round and yet continue to consume even when we have fat stores.

THE FAT IN YOUR BODY

A fat cell is called an adipocyte. A collection of adipocytes is called adipose tissue or just plain fat. A single typical fat cell is about 0.1 millimetre in diameter.

Most of us believe that fat cells just lie around inert, not really contributing to anything other than to our size. This is not true. Fat is, in fact, almost like an endocrine organ releasing hormones, creating inflammation, contributing to immune function and causing you to crave more food. Fat cells are also a storehouse of energy. Fat can be used as fuel for certain functions, especially when glucose from carbohydrates is not available. Fat is especially valuable in fuelling long- duration, low-intensity activity.

Fat cells release certain substances called adipokines and cytokines, which cause inflammation in the body. Fat cells also release the hormone leptin. When there is adequate fat within the fat cells, leptin is released, causing satiety and preventing you from eating more food. Besides leptin, fat cells also produce the reproductive hormones, estrogen and androgens. A deregulation of these hormones in obesity is partly the reason for infertility in some obese subjects.

THE FAT CELL

Fat is thus not really inert matter. It is highly functional, although not always in a positive way.

So what happens to the fat in our body when we exercise?

I am sure we all wonder what exactly happens to the fat when we exercise and 'burn' it? Where does it go and what happens to it?

Chemically, this is what happens—fat gets converted into carbon dioxide and water.

The carbon dioxide gets excreted in our breath (we breathe out CO_2) and the water is excreted in our urine, sweat and feces. Yes, we actually excrete the fat from our body in the form of carbon dioxide and water. For the fat molecule to covert to carbon dioxide and water, however, it has to go through a series of reactions that is possible only when the fat is utilized for energy as happens during exercise, when the heart rate increases. In other words, we have to actually work/be physically active or exercise to convert the fat into carbon dioxide and water. Just breathing heavily or sitting in a sauna won't do it.

Fat cells can undergo increase in size (called hypertrophy) and sometimes increase in numbers (called hyperplasia). The increase in number (hyperplasia) happens particularly in adolescence. Following this stage, the number of cells essentially remain the same and there is usually only an increase in size when we consume too much food or exercise/move too little. That is unless the intake is in such excess that the cells actually multiply in numbers.

The maximum increase in the number of fat cells occurs at the time of puberty in young girls. This is an important observation. At the time, a young girl is going through her menarche or puberty, an excess build-up of fat cells can occur due to poor lifestyle habits. A sudden spurt in fat accumulation is sometimes seen in these young girls.

The new fat cells remain for life.

They may increase or decrease in size depending on energy intake and expenditure but the collective number of cells usually remain constant. That is her legacy. It, therefore, needs to be addressed and controlled in adolescence.

Young girls tend to amass fatty deposits in the breasts and hips, especially during adolescence. That is the normal physiological event preparing a young girl's body for future pregnancy, breast-feeding, and so on. There needs to be a limit to the number of fat cells gained at this point, however. It is easy to go over this threshold and gain excess fat at this point. Teenagers go through several hormonal and physiological changes which may induce mood swings, depression and eating disorders like binging or at the other end of the spectrum, anorexia.

Encouraging her to be extremely active physically through her teenage years ensures that she does not amass too many fat cells that will be her liability through life. Staying physical through the teenage years will build muscle as well. This counteracts the energy intake and restricts the fat-cell accumulation.

Once the number of fat cells is established in adolescence, increase in calorie intake in adulthood tends to increase the size (not the number) of each cell. When we lose fat with exercise and diet, the size (not the number) of the cell shrinks. Essentially we are stuck with the number of fat cells we accumulate in adolescence. We can only control their size. The surgeon's knife is the only way to actually remove fat cells.

A fat cell contains a triglyceride or a molecule of glycerol with three fatty acids attached. Most of the fat cells are present just below the skin, known as subcutaneous fat. Some fat is also seen around some vital organs and is called visceral fat.

TYPES OF BODY FAT

» **White Adipose Tissue**
White adipose tissue is what we commonly see as subcutaneous and visceral fat. An adult may have as many as **three billion fat cells** in her body. This number can increase initially in size and sometimes in number if energy intake is excessive. The increase can be as much as fourfold by division of the original cell if the energy intake is excessive.

» **Brown Adipose Tissue (BAT)**
BAT is known such because of its colour, which appears to be the result of a large number of mitochondria present in these particular fat cells. Brown adipose tissue is not as abundant as the white fat, especially in adults. Babies and hibernating animals seem to have more BAT, especially between their shoulder blades, neck and chest. The main function of BAT seems to be to increase body temperature and keep the baby or animal warm.

A benefit of BAT is its ability to draw triglycerides from the blood stream to fuel itself and also utilize blood glucose for its energy needs. It behaves almost like muscle in that sense.

It was originally thought that adults don't have any brown fat; that they outgrow it once they get past babyhood. As it happens, however, many leaner adults seem to retain some of their brown fat; this has been recognized using PET-CT scans and MRIs. People living in colder climates also appear to have a higher percentage of BAT.

Brown fat burns more calories. It seems an exciting proposition therefore, to find means of increasing the

BAT in our body in order to burn more calories. This is a large area of sensational research (as is most research surrounding weight loss). As peculiar as it sounds, BAT may be a way of combating obesity.

> You can generate more brown fat or BAT by exercising, getting good-quality sleep and exposing yourself to cold climate, such as working out outdoors in cold weather. Lack of exposure to temperature variations could also restrict BAT. So perhaps keeping the central heating revved up is not the best way to stimulate BAT. In other words, allow yourself exposure to natural temperature variations.

A minimal requirement of fat cells is necessary for the human body to function properly. The total amount of fat we carry is measured as a fat percentage. Fat-percentage machines are available in most gyms. Though not 100 per cent accurate, they can be relied upon to give you an idea of how much fat you are carrying. More accurate methods of measuring fat in the body is by using hydrostatic weighing or Dual Energy X-ray Absorptiometry (DEXA).

ACE Chart of Fat Percentage		
Description	Women	Men
Essential fat	10-13%	2-8%
Athletes	14-20%	6-13%
Fitness	21-24%	14-17%
Average	25-31%	18-24%
Obese	Above 32%	Above 25%

IMPORTANT FUNCTIONS OF FAT IN THE BODY

»   The main function of fat is to act as a **storehouse of energy**. Each gram of fat contains and provides 9 calories. The fat cells store fat in the form of triglycerides which when released and metabolized can provide the necessary energy.

»   Fats **absorb vitamins**. There are certain fat-soluble vitamins namely vitamins A, D, E and K. These can only be absorbed from the food if there is fat in the diet. One can, therefore, become deficient in these vitamins if there is inadequate intake of fat. A deficiency of these vitamins is likely to cause problems with vision, bone, blood viscosity, immunity, dry skin and so on.

»   Fats are responsible for the **synthesis and functioning of certain hormones, like the reproductive hormones**. Having too little fat, as seen in some extremely underweight teenage girls, delays puberty. Delayed or absent periods is also common following extremely low-calorie, starvation diets that result in tremendous weight loss. Fats are also an essential part of substances called **prostaglandins** in the body that are necessary for various bodily processes such as constriction or dilatation of blood vessels, contraction of the uterus in labour and so on.

»   Fat provides some **insulation against the cold**. The subcutaneous fat (under the surface of the skin) keeps the body warm and acts like a protective thermal layer in cold weather.

»   Fat is important as part of the **structural component of nerves and cell membranes.**

»   Fat is essential to keep the **hair and skin healthy.** Dry, flaky skin is often a result of a deficiency of essential fats.

All the above functions can be well taken care of with a limited amount of fat in the body. As seen in the fat-percentage chart given, a value above 32 per cent is considered obese. One needs to try to remain within the normal range for the given age. Athletes who spend a fair amount of time training and focusing on their nutrition have a lower fat percentage of about 14 to 20 per cent. Most women should try and sustain a 24 per cent fat percentage if fit. With age it is expected that the fat percentage rises but it should be sustained below 30 per cent.

Astonishingly, about 90 per cent of the women I have assessed have a fat percentage of 30 per cent and above. Even the ones who 'appear' slim seem to have a high fat percentage. The primary reason for this is that they don't build enough muscle. Their focus on cardio and diet alone does not get to the root of the problem, which is the low muscle mass or **sarcopenia.**

In excess, fat begins to create problems within the body. An increase in the size of the body is only one of the problems. A lowered level of self-esteem, poorer quality of life, difficulty in performing even minor tasks like climbing stairs, lower productivity, depression, diabetes, hypertension, cancer, heart disease, increased incidence of falls, injury, poor recovery following surgery or infection are only some of the problems faced.

The role of exercise and diet in fat loss to improve the quality of life is highly underestimated.

I have spoken to hundreds of women from various walks of life. Doctors, women in corporate jobs, social groups, young mothers, pregnant women, housewives, and many more. The most common reason too many of them have still not incorporated exercise into their lives is the claim that they have no time. I believe it is more likely that they do not particularly think an hour of exercise is worth their time. They always seem to have something more important to do.

Life, however, passes you by and before you know it, age catches up along with a host of illnesses that one spends a large part of one's day dealing with. What then is the point of wealth or even time at a later stage when one's body has degenerated?

A patient was talking to me about a detox farm she had been to. A magical place where they massage you, give you enemas, make you drink a lot of fluids, eat vegetarian and subject you to a variety of treatments. Your body apparently needs all of this to be rid of the toxins that it has accumulated. These toxins apparently cause you to gain weight.

Besides being prohibitively expensive, these detox centres are a huge marketing gig that many people buy into.

Do you know the best detox the body has are *sweat*, *urine* and *faeces*?

The body is quite capable of detoxing itself if you treat it well and keep it running with healthy food and exercise. You certainly do not need any special treatments to detox. Ask yourself this simple, common-sense question:

After this wonderful detox that has happened over a period of perhaps a week, how does one sustain this clean detoxed body over the next couple of months?

Of course, the people at the farm insist you need it every couple of months, so that clarifies things up a bit.

If you want to pamper yourself with massages, want to be told what to eat and drink, even have it measured out for you, want to wallow in mud baths and oil wells, go ahead and enjoy it. **Do not label it detoxing and insult the brilliantly engineered human body, which is far more sophisticated than that.**

Sometimes it helps to get some perspective.

Recap

- Fat, like all the other major nutrients, is an essential part of your diet as it has certain functions to perform in the body.
- Beware of 'fat free' foods, they may not necessarily be low in calories.
- There are different kinds of fat—Saturated and Unsaturated (MUFA and PUFA)
- The excess fat is stored in your body within cells called adipocytes.
- As we accumulate more fat through our diet (and decreased calorie expenditure), the excess causes the already existing fat cells to expand rather than

multiply. The cells multiply primarily at the time of puberty. These cells remain for life.

- There is a minimum and maximum fat percentage that is advisable for human beings, depending on gender, age and fitness levels.

11

A DAY IN THE LIFE OF FLUFFY, THE FAT CELL

How Increasing Muscle Helps Burn Fat?

Fluffy is a fat molecule, the universal adversary in today's day and age. We all have a certain level of distress and anguish about the presence of Fluffy in our body. Fact is, Fluffy has certain functions and if life is lead judiciously with the adequate amount of exercise, functioning of muscles and a reasonable intake of food, then Fluffy functions quite normally and has a role to play.

Here I will explain how it is primarily the muscle cells that utilize Fluffy. This makes it imperative therefore that we have an adequate amount of muscle cells. We come back once again to the theory, **gain muscle to lose fat.**

Fluffy is a fat molecule that floats down the blood stream after a fatty meal. It is carried to the fat cell or adipocyte by the blood stream. Following a meal, the hormone insulin rises, enabling the transfer and storage of Fluffy within the adipocyte.

Fluffy resides within the adipocyte of the fat cell, which is present either under the skin (subcutaneous fat) or around the important organs (visceral fat).

Adipocytes are the storehouses for Fluffy. Inside the adipocyte Fluffy is present as triacylglycerol or TAG.

When there is a demand for energy, for instance during exercise, Fluffy is released from the adipocyte back into the blood stream. This is aided by the hormone epinephrine (or adrenalin). Epinephrine causes the TAG bond to break and the fatty acids to be released. These fatty acids travel through the blood attached to a protein called albumin, as they are not soluble directly in the water-based blood.

Dismembered Fluffy (by now only the fatty acids remain) is taken to the muscles through the small blood vessels traversing the muscle cells.

It crosses through the wall of the blood vessel (the endothelium) and through the wall of the muscle cell (the sarcolemma) and into the muscle itself. Two interesting binding proteins, called FAT/CD36 and FABPpm, aid this process.

Once inside the muscle cell a molecule called Coenzyme A (CoA) is added to Fluffly.

Fluffy with CoA can have two different fates depending on the circumstances:

- It can be stored within the muscle cell as Intra Muscular Triacylglycerol (IMTAG). IMTAG acts as a source of energy when the muscle requires it for endurance activities like long-duration exercise.

  A very small percentage of the body's fat is stored

as IMTAG, however.

- Alternately, Fluffy with CoA can undergo a process called oxidation (where electrons are removed from a molecule) when energy is required for the working of the muscle.

In order for oxidation to take place, Fluffy, along with CoA must be transported to the cell's power plant, which is the mitochondria, the fat-burning furnace in the cell. The carnitine shuttle supports this transport into the mitochondria. (Think of it like the shuttle that transports you from one terminal of an airport to another.)

Inside the mitochondria, Fluffy loses electrons. These electrons are transported by the electron-transport chain for further oxidation and the production of energy with the release of ATP or adenosine triphosphate for the contraction of the muscle. The remaining unused energy becomes heat energy to sustain body temperature.

All of this requires a constant supply of oxygen, hence this process is called aerobic metabolism.

As you can see, all of this happens within the mitochondria of the muscle cell.

A trained individual with more muscle mass is better able to utilize fat as a source of energy. Having more muscle mass also means she needs more energy, which is released from the fat stores.

- A trained individual with more muscle mass will better transport of fatty acids cross the membranes into the muscle cells.

- A trained individual has more microvasculature or small blood vessels within the muscles, making the transport of fatty acids easier.
- They also show an increased number of mitochondria within each muscle cell.
- Interestingly, the IMTAG stores within the muscle cells of these individuals also appear to be closer to the mitochondria, making the transfer easier.

So what does all this mean?

It means that burning fat or using fat for energy is a complicated and intricate process that happens primarily in the muscle cell. The muscular component of the body is the one that uses the largest amount of energy. There is something called the resting energy expenditure or REE, which is the energy the body uses even while at rest. Increasing the amount of muscle can maximize this REE. During exercise the energy utilized by the muscles is even more. One of the important ways of keeping weight gain in check and losing fat is to increase the muscle mass, since muscles are the primary consumers of energy from the fat stores (in the form of Fluffy).

It stands to reason therefore, that the more muscle cells there are, the more fat gets utilized. Gain more muscle to lose more fat.

Recap

- Fluffy the fat cell resides in the adipocyte.
- It is called upon for fuel by the muscle cells, especially when there is poor availability of glucose.

- Through a complicated series of reactions, the fat enters the muscle cell where it is either stored or used for energy.
- This conversion to energy takes place within the 'powerhouse' of the muscle cell or the Mitochondria to produce ATP, which is necessary for the contraction (working) of muscle.
- It goes to show therefore, that the greater your muscle mass, the more your fat will be utilized for energy.
- Build more muscle—burn more fat

12

CARBOHYDRATES AND PROTEINS

Their Metabolism, Exercise and Fat Loss

CARBOHYDRATES IN YOUR DIET

Carbohydrates form a major part of our diet. Carbohydrates can be found mostly in whole grains, fruits and vegetables. Beans, lentils, peas, corn and potatoes also contain high percentages of carbohydrates although the beans and lentils form a major source of protein as well, especially in the vegetarian diet. Most foods are a combination of many food groups and may contain varying quantities of carbohydrates, protein and fats in addition to the vitamins and minerals.

Carbohydrates are broadly divided into **simple and complex carbohydrates and fibre.**

SIMPLE CARBOHYDRATES OR SUGARS

These are to be found naturally in milk (as lactose) and fruit (as fructose). Added sugars are processed forms of sucrose seen in table sugar and syrups. Simple carbohydrates are usually added to food to enhance flavour (and calories). They often go unrecognized as they are not visible to the naked eye. All carbohydrates do, however, supply 4 calories/gram.

COMPLEX CARBOHYDRATESS OR STARCHES

Whole grains like unpolished rice, oats and barley have three parts:

» The outer bran
» The germ
» The endosperm

The outer bran or outer shell has the fibre along with Vitamin B and minerals.

The germ in the next layer consists of valuable nutrients like the fatty acids and Vitamin E.

The endosperm is the innermost kernel and contains the starch.

When grains are polished or refined, much of the outer layers are removed and what remains is primarily the starchy endosperm.

DIETARY FIBRE

Dietary fibres are found in fruits, vegetables, whole grains, nuts and legumes. Fibre is further divided into:

» *Insoluble Fibre*: This kind of fibre is essentially unabsorbed when eaten and passes right through your intestines to form the bulk of the stool. This is found mainly in the outer husk of whole grains, seeds, nuts and vegetables.

» *Soluble Fibre*: These fibres, on the other hand, that are found in oats, apples, pears, flax seed berries, etc., are absorbed and have the unique property of lowering cholesterol levels in the blood.

CARBOHYDRATES IN YOUR BODY

When consumed, carbohydrates from food get broken down into glucose, absorbed from the small intestines and into the blood stream. After a meal, when blood-glucose concentrations increase, insulin is secreted from the pancreas to stimulate transfer of glucose from the blood into the cells of the liver or muscles. This is in order to sustain the blood-glucose levels on an even keel (unless you are diabetic and have a defective level of insulin secretion or response).

If the muscles are working, as in during activity or exercise, the glucose gets shunted into them to be utilized as a source of fuel. If the muscles are at rest, the glucose moves into the liver for storage and later use. The storage form of glucose is glycogen. The formation of glycogen from glucose is called *glycogenesis* or *anabolism*.

When blood-sugar levels drop, several hours after a meal, the hormones glucagon and epinephrine are secreted from the pancreas to convert the glycogen from the liver back into glucose (once again to keep blood-sugar levels on an even keel). This process is called *glycogenolysis* or *catabolism*. The catabolic process produces a substance called **Adenosine Triphosphate** (ATP), which is the actual fuel necessary for the contraction of the muscles.

HOW CARBOHYDRATES ARE USED FOR ENERGY IN OUR BODY?

The primary metabolic pathway for the formation of ATP is through what is called the **citric acid cycle or the krebs cycle.**

As already seen in the previous chapter, ATP or the currency for fuel is also produced from fat cells. The rate of production from the fat cell is, however, very slow and therefore can only be used to fuel low-intensity exercise. When muscles work at a low intensity, the fat from the fat cells (Fluffy) is transported to the muscle for breakdown and energy. This is especially so when the glucose levels in the blood, muscle and liver are low, which happens when fasting or several hours after a meal.

This is one of the reasons why the term 'fat-burning zone' was coined for exercise done at a low to moderate intensity. It is also the reason why working out on an empty stomach taps into the body's fat stores. Recall though, that it is the **total number of calories burnt and the energy balance** at the end of the day/week/month that eventually determines weight loss.

For instance, let's say you exercise on an empty stomach or at a low to moderate pace (the so-called 'fat-burning zone') believing you are burning up your fat. You then proceed to have a huge breakfast. The energy consumed will outweigh the energy expended irrespective of whether it came from your fat or the blood glucose. It is a **consistently lower-calorie intake as opposed to expenditure** that eventually leads to weight loss. In a exercise of moderate intensity, where the muscles work harder, as in a brisk walk, the fat is unable to supply the ATP as fuel fast enough. The body has to depend on stored glycogen or glucose from a meal and the continuous supply of oxygen for this level of exercise to be maintained. Obviously then, this level of intensity cannot be sustained for long as the energy source (the glycogen) runs out.

Consuming carbohydrates is essential for the supply of glucose and therefore energy, for the muscles to function especially during higher-intensity, shorter-duration exercise. In long-duration, low-intensity exercise, fats can be used as a source of energy.

When large quantities of carbohydrates are consumed, they are converted to the storage form glycogen to be deposited in the liver. When intake continues to rise without the stored glycogen being utilized, however the liver converts the glycogen to triglycerides or fatty acids to be stored in the fat cells.

Ultimately, the result of overconsumption of carbohydrates is conversion to fat.

ARE CARBOHYDRATES BAD FOR YOU? WHAT ABOUT LOW-CARBOHYDRATE DIETS?

Carbohydrates are certainly not bad for you. It is the excess of carbohydrates amounting to excess in calories that will pile on the kilos and eventually affect health. Low-carbohydrate diets, which recommend reducing carbohydrates drastically from your diet, do in fact lower the weight. The reasons seem to be complex.

Some of the hypotheses are:

» A greater satiety level when more protein (especially animal protein) is consumed. You tend to feel full faster and for longer.

» The digestion of protein is itself more energy-consuming thereby burning more calories.

» Low-carbohydrate diets are also sometimes lower-calorie diets, enabling weight loss.

» On a high-protein diet the body starts to use fat as a source of energy instead of carbohydrates going into a metabolic state called ketogenesis. As result of ketogenesis, the excess production of ketone bodies in the body dulls the appetite and often causes nausea and bad breath. You end up eating less.

Removing carbohydrates completely or going on a very-low-carbohydrate diet can have other problems like deficiency of essential nutrients. How long one can withstand such a diet is also questionable.

Several different cultures around the world including Southeast Asia, New Guinea Highland tribe at Tukisenta consume much larger proportions of carbohydrates and remain lean. Obesity in these areas seems to have risen after the inclusion of refined foods, flour and sugar coupled with a decrease in physical activity. The problem, therefore, is not just the consumption of carbohydrates alone but also the result of a decrease in energy expenditure and affluence (a lazier lifestyle), leading to indulgence in higher calorie, refined, processed foods.

Refined carbohydrates, made highly palatable with the addition of sugar, fats, salt, and other additives encourage overeating. This kind of food is highly gratifying and addictive, effectively leading to severe cravings. Consuming colas, fruit juice, sweetened cereals, and snacking on sweetened chocolate and power bars lead to an enormous accumulation of calorie intake and eventually fat gain.

How much carbohydrate intake an individual requires is highly varied and often has to be arrived at after trial and error. Some people feel perfectly fine with consuming 40 to 60 per cent of their calories from carbohydrates as recommended by most balanced diets and the food pyramid. In this case, the amount of protein would need to be about 20 to 30 per cent and fat intake, another 15 to 30 per cent of calories.

If the weight remains unchanged, you feel energetic, can exercise regularly and remain active through the day, your diet can be assumed to be balanced.

If, on the other hand, you feel lethargic, low on energy, sleepy and unable to exercise or even stay active, then you are probably consuming too much.

Some people find their weight starts coming off only when they lower their carbohydrate intake to less than 40 per cent and increase their protein to 30 to 40 per cent and maintain their fats at about 30 per cent. If they feel healthy with this dietary modification, exercise regularly, are able to build muscle and stay energetic through the day, the diet is probably working for them.

There are studies confirming that weight loss appears to be more pronounced when more protein and fat and lesser carbohydrates are used as opposed to a low-fat, moderate-protein and higher-carbohydrate diet. This, however, is in the short term. Proponents of Atkins and Paleo diets would, of course swear to this.

However, is such a diet suitable for all?

I don't think so.

It is neither practical nor sustainable in the long term for many. Adjustment of carbohydrates has to happen on an individual basis. However, there are small changes one can make to optimize the carbohydrate intake. Choose your carbohydrates wisely.

Instead of	Choose
• Polished rice	• Red, brown or unpolished rice
• White bread made from refined flour	• Whole grain, multigrain bread
• Sugary drinks like sweetened fruit juice	• Whole fruit with its fibre
• Fried potato chips	• Baked or roasted potatoes
• Colas and other drinks	• Plain water

Following up with the biochemical and hormonal profile of your blood to identify cholesterol, sugar, thyroid levels and kidney function is also a wise idea to ensure that the diet you are on is also working well internally.

Sometimes, you may be losing weight but causing damage to your kidneys or heart by following highly rigid diets that exclude or drastically increase any one macro nutrient.

CARBOHYDRATES AS A SOURCE OF ENERGY FOR MUSCLES

Dietary carbohydrates supply glucose to the working muscles. Glucose is also stored as glycogen within the muscle cells and in the liver. The blood glucose and/or stored glycogen undergo glycolysis to produce ATP and energy when required.

If the intensity of the exercise is lower than 50 per cent (slow jogging, walking, day-to-day activities, physical labour) fat can be used as a source of ATP and this activity, therefore, can be continued for a long time (as most of us do have adequate amounts of fat to fuel several days of low-intensity activity). However, as the level of intensity of exercise rises, the fats cannot provide the energy at an adequate rate and the stored carbohydrates are then required.

THE THREE ENERGY SYSTEMS FOR THE PRODUCTION OF ATP

Under different conditions ATP is produced in different ways. There are essentially three systems that produce this end result.

» ATP-CP system
» Aerobic pathway
» Anaerobic pathway

THE ATP-CP SYSTEM OR THE PHOSPHAGEN SYSTEM (FOR SPRINTING OR OTHER HIGH INTENSITY, SHORT DURATION EXERCISE)

This system is an energy pathway that supplies ATP when energy is required for very short periods of time. It could, for instance, support a 100-metre sprint. The ATP used comes from the small quantities already stored within muscle cells. Once that is used up, creatinin phosphate (CP) is used to resynthesize ATP. Both these processes supply energy for about ten seconds of an all-out activity or exercise at maximum intensity. Thereafter, if the body continues to exercise, the supply of ATP has to come through the aerobic or anaerobic pathways.

ANAEROBIC PATHWAY OR GLYCOLYTIC SYSTEM (FOR WEIGHT TRAINING)

This system provides ATP from glucose through a process of gycolysis. It does not depend on the constant supply of oxygen. The by-product of the production of ATP through this pathway is lactic acid. This system supports high-intensity activity for short periods of time of a few minutes. At the end of this time, the accumulation of lactic acid within the muscle cells leads to muscle pain (the burn) and fatigue. This essentially means that the muscles reach their lactate threshold. Weight training and running at fairly high speeds (levels below sprinting but above jogging) fall into this category. You can continue the exercise until the muscles begin to scream with the lactic acid build-up.

AEROBIC PATHWAY (FOR LONGER-DURATION CARDIO)

The energy produced when the body is working at a low to moderate intensity, or even resting is through the aerobic system or oxidative system. This system can supply ATP or energy indefinitely (at least for prolonged periods of time) as in low-intensity, long-duration activities like a long trek or a low-intensity marathon.

This system is entirely dependent on the constant supply of oxygen (hence the name) to break down nutrients (carbohydrates, protein and fats) to produce ATP. In this pathway, carbohydrates are not the only source of energy. Both fats and proteins can enter the citric acid cycle to produce energy via ATP.

CARBOHYDRATES AND INSULIN

It is widely believed that there is a connection between the secretion of insulin and the increased storage of fat. One of the roles of insulin is to prevent lipolysis or the breakdown of fat. Insulin is secreted after a meal. It not only regulates blood sugar by aiding the shunting of glucose into the liver and cells but also prevents the breakdown of fat from the fat cells. Naturally, therefore, it was assumed that an increase of insulin causes fat gain. The hormone has acquired a ruthless reputation in this regard.

However, the rise of insulin is strictly restricted to the post-prandial period. The fat that was not broken down during that small window has every opportunity to do so when the levels of insulin decline, as they should several hours after a meal and can be utilized later, provided one presents the right opportunity (work, activity, exercise).

If the muscles are working (during exercise or activity), the energy required for a low-intensity activity comes from the fat cells as already explained. As long as one eats in moderation and continues to work out and stay active, then the energy gets balanced and the individual does not gain fat.

I hear this so very often—

'I have stopped eating rice. But I am just not losing weight!'

Stopping rice alone is not the solution to weight loss. The Indian cuisine has a lot of alternatives to rice such as rotis, poha, upuma, idlis, dosas and bread, which fundamentally belong to the same food group. If you are over-consuming any of the other items from this food group, believing that deleting rice will solve your problems, you are greatly mistaken.

Calculate serving sizes and evaluate if you are eating within the number of servings recommended for you in order to lose weight.

EVENTUALLY IT COMES DOWN TO ENERGY CONSUMPTION VERSUS EXPENDITURE

One cannot solely blame insulin for fat gain. The combination of excess calories from rich, processed food, decreased physical activity and an environment that encourages an indolent lifestyle with as little movement as possible is the real reason for obesity.

It is true that some people seem to be more prone to obesity. They certainly may not be able to exercise all their weight away. They have a genetic propensity to remain larger. It should not prevent them from exercising regularly and getting fitter, though. Cutting carbohydrate intake has been found to be an effective way to lose weight in such people. The diet has to be managed carefully, however, and adequate carbohydrates reintroduced if necessary. Persisting with exercise is important not just to improve fitness but also to alter the mood and stay motivated. Dieting alone can lead to low energy levels, even depression. This is certainly not an ideal situation for an overweight individual. What one needs is motivation and energy to sustain positive lifestyle changes.

Building muscle to Use the carbohydrates You consume

Muscles use glucose from carbohydrates as their source of energy. The larger the muscles, the more the requirement for glucose as energy and more one can consume.

Glucose is necessary for the functioning of everything including the brain. Muscles are large consumers of glucose as energy and it makes sense to build enough muscle to make use of the consumed carbohydrates. The more muscle you have, the more energy you require from your carbohydrate intake and the more carbohydrates you can consume without gaining fat.

How much better can it get?

PROTEIN

Proteins are one of the major nutrients along with carbohydrates and fats. They are required for various functions in the body and act as building blocks for muscles, antibodies, blood cells (hemoglobin), skin, hair, some enzymes and hormones. Proteins are therefore essential for the functioning of our body. They are made up of amino acids, most of which can be made by the body itself. Some of these amino acids that are not manufactured by the body need to be consumed as food. These are called the *essential amino acids*.

PROTEIN-RICH FOODS

Animal protein are meats, poultry, eggs, milk and fish. Vegetarian proteins are nuts, seeds, legumes and soy.

Most foods contain combinations of carbohydrates, proteins and fats, as already mentioned. Even grains contain amino acids, which, when digested and absorbed by the body, can be used for the synthesis of proteins. Most vegetarian sources of protein, however, are called incomplete proteins since they do not contain all the amino acids required to make protein within the body. Combining foods with different amino acids, therefore, enables the balanced absorption of the required amino acids for protein synthesis.

For example, the combination of rice (which is a grain and contains some amino acids) and beans (which is a legume and is rich in the amino acid absent in rice) is a classic combination consumed for years, which provides the right balance of the required amino acids.

Some ingested amino acids are used for protein biosynthesis, while others are converted to glucose through gluconeogenesis or fed into the citric acid or krebs cycle. In other words, **protein can also be used as a source of fuel, especially when there are no carbohydrates available**. This is what happens during starvation. Due to the absence of glucose from carbohydrates as a source of fuel, the body begins to use its own protein from within the body or its own muscles as a source of energy.

Similarly, in a high-protein and a low- or no-carbohydrate diet, proteins get used as an energy source. The result is a metabolic by-product called ketone bodies.

HOW MUCH PROTEIN DO YOU NEED?

An active individual looking at losing fat and retaining muscle should consume about 1 to 2 g/kg body weight

and combine it with heavy weight training.
A sedentary individual not looking at any change in body composition should be consuming about 0.8 g/kg body weight.

Consuming protein alone will not change body composition. One needs to train with weights to stimulate and grow the muscle while consuming 1 to 2 g/kg protein within your dietary allowance. Remember, every gram of protein supplies 4 kilocalories. A woman weighing 55 kg can consume about 55 grams of protein a day.

Reading through the chapter 'Food For Thought' in *Get Size Wise* will help you understand your protein (and other) requirements better.

Remember that 3 ounces is the equivalent of one serving from the protein group (meat, poultry, lentils, nuts, seeds). Although 3 ounces is approximately 84 grams, a piece of meat weighing 3 ounces will not provide you with exactly 84 grams of protein. Meat has other nutrients too, besides proteins. Therefore, 3 ounces (84 grams) of meat will only provide about 21 grams of protein.

Several studies have shown that keeping your protein intake at about 1.5 g/kg body weight while on a calorie-restricted diet, combined with exercise will maintain lean body mass or muscle. Consuming less protein while on an energy-restricted diet can lead to loss of muscle mass. A higher-protein diet appears to protect the muscles.

EATING ENOUGH PROTEIN

Ensure that you eat beans, nuts and legumes every day. This is especially important when you are training with weights and intend to increase or at least maintain muscle mass.

Restricting your carbohydrate intake to four to six servings a day will enable you to eat more proteins. The problem arises when one fills up on the carbohydrates group (as in most Indian cuisine) and is unable to eat much protein. In a vegetarian diet, it is important to consciously consume protein sources of food.

It may be necessary to supplement protein drinks to ensure adequate protein intake. Most protein supplements are made from casein or whey. Identify a good source and after analysing the quantity of protein you are currently taking, a supplement to make up the rest of the required intake.

IMPORTANCE OF EATING ENOUGH PROTEINS

» Proteins have the highest levels of thermic effect of food or TEF. This is the number of calories burnt just to digest the particular nutrient. The TEF of protein is twenty to thirty-five, which means that 20 to 35 per cent of the energy from the protein is utilized just to digest it effectively. The body therefore, expends a lot more energy in the process of digesting proteins than in digesting carbohydrates or fats.

» Protein stabilizes your energy levels. As proteins take longer to digest they keep you satiated for longer.

» Proteins safeguard against the breakdown of muscle tissue. When on a lower-calorie diet, the body tends to breakdown muscle if it requires amino acids. If the protein intake is sufficient then this assault against the amino acids from muscle tissue is prevented and the muscle is preserved.

» Proteins boost the immune system. Amino acids are essential for the proper functioning of the immune system, keeping you healthier.

Recap

- The ATP-CP system provides energy only for very short, intense bursts of energy like sprints lasting about ten seconds. This depends purely on the ATP and CP stored within the muscle cells and is converted into ATP.

- The anaerobic pathway also produces ATP from the partial breakdown of glycogen but without the need for a supply of oxygen. The system therefore cannot support prolonged activity. The energy supply lasts a few minutes at most.

- The aerobic system depends on the constant supply of oxygen to convert either fats or carbohydrates to provide energy or ATP.

- Consumption of carbohydrates results in an increase of insulin in the immediate post-meal period.

- Building adequate muscle mass aids in the utilization of consumed carbohydrates, fats and protein and minimizes the storage of fat.

13

THE ANTI-AGEING PILL

Reversing the Ageing Process with
Weight Training

We know that disuse leads to deterioration. Use it or lose it. This pertains to both the cerebral and physical self. A lack of intellectual, emotional or spiritual stimulus leads to considerable and rapid degeneration of the mind. Everything including your memory requires to be challenged regularly in order for it to remain responsive. Apathy only slows you down further. Similarly, with the physical body, neglect eventually results in the atrophy of the muscles and degeneration of the joints, ligaments, bones and tendons.

It leads to:

» Fat accumulation
» Muscle atrophy
» A reduction in stamina, strength and flexibility

You become a mass of aches and pains. Mobility is limited. Independence is lost. Depression sets in as a result of the feeling of inadequacy and lack of freedom of movement.

Most elderly people lose confidence in themselves, as they fear falling down, injury and further infirmity. However, most people are resigned to these changes as being part of the 'normal ageing process'. It doesn't have to be this way. Althought today, life expectancy in India about sixty-seven to sixty-nine years (Union Ministry of Health and Family Welfare), no one questions the quality of life.

In order to lead a higher-quality life, one needs to remain physically healthy, mobile and independent.

Ageing is a natural process. One cannot truly prevent it from happening as time marches resolutely on. What one can do, however, is to age gracefully in the best possible manner that is available to you. I don't mean you have to cling, kicking and screaming, to the doors of your youth, but clearly, taking good care of the body (and mind) keeps it youthful, yet allows for maturity and wisdom.

Loss of muscle (or atrophy) is a well-known and debilitating result of ageing and disuse. Sedentary living and lack of physical exercise, especially exercise against external resistance (as in strength training), eventually leads to sarcopenia or decrease in muscle mass. Given that Indians already suffer from this condition, this is a disastrous predicament. With age, muscle atrophy escalates leading to poor mobility and decreased functionality. The muscles themselves age.

In a study done by Simon Melov et al, in 2007, they found that regular weight training for six months leads to several changes in both the older and younger people studied:

» The muscle size increased
» The muscle strength improved

» The genetic expression within individual muscle cells was altered

WHAT DOES THIS MEAN?

A gene is a basic functional unit of heredity of a living organism. Genes form a part of our DNA and can be made up of several hundred or million DNA units. Twenty-five to thirty-five thousand genes are present in every one of the cells in our body, including the muscle cells.

Genes determine various things about the human body. Your distinct genes, which you have inherited from both your parents, determine your unique physical qualities, such as the colour of your skin, texture of your hair, the colour of your eyes, your height, and so on. The genes present in the muscle determine the age of the muscle, wear and tear, ability to increase in size and strength.

In the study by S. Melov et al, following six months of resistance/strength training, aside from the obvious physical appearance of bigger, stronger muscles, several changes were found at the genetic level. On microscopic evaluation of the muscle biopsies, several genes within the muscles studied were found to be enriched and the signs of ageing were reversed. This would mean that not only did the muscles appear visibly larger, firmer and stronger, but they were also genetically younger at a basic cellular level.

MOST COMMON AILMENTS PLAGUING OLDER WOMEN

» Diabetes
» Hypertension
» Osteoporosis

» Obesity
» Falls and injury
» Depression
» Loss of confidence as a result of loss of strength and balance

All the above (and more) can be prevented and treated with the right weight-training schedule. Weight training therefore, is an essential aspect of fitness if you want to keep your body looking youthful inside out. If the above explanation, of the intricate workings of the body benefiting from strength was not enough to convince you, here's what is clearly obvious to the naked eye —

Strength training can be viewed as an anti-ageing pill of sorts.

What do we see typically happen with age?

Sagging flesh, even if this is not seen in excess, does occur. Fat does not hold up well to gravity. As a result, thighs, stomach, bottom and arms, common areas that are usually covered with layers of fat, tend to sag. The solution is to burn the fat and build muscle instead. Muscle is closely adherent to bone and denser in consistency than fat. Thus the body looks more youthful and toned.

Most treatments to look younger propagate expensive creams, botox, lifts and tucks. Not to mention supplements, highly expensive investigative procedures, surgery, foods that promise eternal youth (no doubt prohibitive) and many more clever ploys that seem to attract women. Why is it that we always want to find another contorted path when clearly there is already one available? All the above only bring about superficial transformations (if they do anything at all). What about the physiology, biochemistry and the internal workings of the body? How does one keep that young and healthy? Strength training has been largely overlooked as a tool to build a better body — from both the physical and the physiological perspectives.

PHYSIOLOGICAL REVERSAL OF AGEING

Strength training has been found to alter other biochemical markers in the body —

» Blood sugar levels are better controlled
» Cholesterol is improved
» Blood pressure is reduced
» Tone of the muscle tone is improved
» Abdominal fat is reduced
» Mineral density of bones is improved, preventing osteoporosis

All the above are the most common consequences of the ageing process. Training with weights can reverse all of them, keeping you not only looking, but also feeling and truly being younger.

Mrs Devaram is a feisty 72 year old that can put a thirty year old to shame. Meeting her was a real pleasure indeed. Her main concerns were how to get fitter, how to lose the tiny bit of flab around her waist, and how to increase muscle mass! Age IS really just a number. There are young women in their twenties who are unfit and overweight. For all practical purposes they could well be sixty. Then there are women like Mrs Devaram who could very well be thirty!

Recap

- Disuse of muscle (as with everything else) leads to deterioration.
- One of the greatest benefits of weight training to build strength and muscle mass is to improve daily functionality, especially with older women.
- Brilliant research has actually shown that weight training creates changes within the genetic material of the muscle cells, changing our very genetic makeup and expression, reversing the signs of aging!
- Weight training may be therefore seen as a very powerful anti-aging therapy making one youthful both externally (firm toned muscles) and internally (our DNA).

14

STAYING STRONG WITH AGE

Strength Training at Various Stages in Life

CHILDREN AND ADOLESCENTS

At one time it was thought that resistance training or weight training (using one's own body weight or external weights like dumb-bells, barbells) was unsafe for children and adolescents. This theory was based on research done in Japan on child labourers that found these children to be of below-average size. It was concluded that this was the result of lifting heavy objects at a very young age. This theory was not questioned. Neither was the possibility that nutrition perhaps played a major role in their growth restriction. Thus, it became a well-established myth that children and adolescents should not train against resistance. That is, they should not train with weights.

Recent research, however, has disproved this theory and it has been found that resistance training can be a safe, effective and worthwhile activity for children and adolescents, provided it is supervised and monitored by qualified professionals.

> Children as young as eight to nine can start with own-body-weight exercises like push-ups, squats, pull-ups, lunges, and so on. Hanging on monkey bars, climbing ropes and trees, jumping up and down from levels at various heights, improves strength in the concerned muscles. A gradual progression can be made to include external weights like light dumb-bells, resistance bands and weighted balls.
>
> The resistance exercise needs to be kept at a moderate load with higher repetitions rather than a heavier load with lower repetitions.

Interestingly, children who train against resistance do not necessarily build muscle or bulk up. What this training seems to do is make the necessary, important neuronal connections between the brain and the muscle fibres. **An increase in strength, not size**, of the muscles is seen. It appears that the training activates the innate strength that the muscle is capable of. It ensures that as many muscle fibres as possible are stimulated and innervated by nerves. The true functionality of the muscles is thus sustained. If the resistance training is continued into adulthood, it ensures that the all-important muscles remain highly effective in keeping the body mobile and healthy.

In today's world it is not just adults that are immobile and incapable of performing physical labour. Children sit, staring at the television as soon as they can begin focusing. The Internet, smartphones and computer games have replaced actual physical activity. As a result the body develops peculiarly. Balance, gait, speed, agility, reflexes, power, posture and a whole host of other naturally available physical skills are compromised. Strength and the appropriate development of muscles can be accomplished with resistance training.

I think this is particularly important for a young girl. Being physically stronger builds her confidence and she starts disbelieving the very existence of the 'weaker sex' at a young age. She also begins to build enough muscle at a young age, bracing her body to handle the various physiological changes, like puberty, pregnancy and menopause, that it has to endure.

Make exercising fun for kids. It does not necessarily have to be a physical training drill. Props like Swiss balls, weighted balls, resistance bands, steppers, hula hoops make for a more interesting workout. When this is initiated in early childhood and nurtured throughout life, it becomes a natural progression, an accepted part of one's daily living unlike what it is now.

TWENTIES AND THIRTIES

Weight training should be an essential part of a fitness routine for these young women. They need to develop an enduring foundation of muscle mass to take them through the rest of their lives. Preventing fat gain as they age then becomes possible. Most women get pregnant and have children in these decades. Having a strong body makes the journey easier.

However, these seem to be the decades when women are terribly obsessed with their appearance rather than functionality or health. They put their bodies through cycles of dieting and cardio to 'lose weight'. As a result, they also lose muscle. They then set themselves up to gain fat as they age, as they have lost the critical component (muscle) that maintains a higher BMR.

PREGNANCY

Weight training in pregnancy is certainly not contraindicated, particularly if you have been training with weights before being pregnant.

During your pregnancy the objective of weight training is not to lift progressively heavier weights but to maintain muscle mass and strength. The correct breathing technique and proper form of exercise has to be strictly adhered to. Common ailments of pregnancy like back pain, excessive lumbar lordosis or arching of the lower spine, slouched shoulders with the weight of the breasts, and so on can be circumvented by strengthening the associated muscles. The hormone relaxin causes some hypermobility of joints during pregnancy. Care needs to be taken, therefore, while exercising (weight training, stretching or cardio) to prevent injury.

A woman who has trained before her pregnancy will have better body awareness, strength and coordination while exercising. This helps her avoid injury. One who has never exercised before may face some problems, as her lack of body awareness will contribute to injury if she is not guided or monitored properly.

I find most women who have been training with weights stop once they get pregnant. While you could lower the weight used depending on the stage of your pregnancy, it is not necessary to stop altogether.

The usual precautions to be taken while exercising in pregnancy have to be followed:

» Do not exercise if you are unwell or have a fever.
» Stop if you feel dizzy or light headed.
» Never strain or hold your breath.
» Do not lie flat on your back after the fourth month of pregnancy.
» Keep yourself well hydrated.
» Avoid extreme of temperature or humidity.
» Avoid injury from dropping weights on yourself.
» Do not exercise if there are complications in pregnancy, like hypertension, preeclampsia, bleeding, threatened abortion and so on.
» Keep your doctor informed and updated.

Pregnancy is a time when women seem to become more conscious of their health and seem to want to incorporate healthy behaviour. Many antenatal programmes insist that one should only do 'gentle exercises' like yoga and avoid weight training. Let me emphasize again, yoga and other antenatal practices like meditation, relaxation and breathing are not the only kind of exercises one should do through pregnancy. Doing them should not prevent you from strengthening yourself with weights as well. The two are not counterproductive. In fact, balancing strength training with yoga stretches, breathing and meditation work very well together to improve the pregnant months. The key is to be monitored and guided correctly.

Sure, you can injure yourself with weights – if done incorrectly. Just as you can injure yourself with any kind of exercise, including yoga, when done incorrectly.

Clearly, pregnancy is not a time to start working out

maniacally. It is, however, a time to become more aware of one's health and try to absorb practices that can be carried through post delivery.

POST DELIVERY

Women gain up to 10 to 20 kg in their pregnancy. Much of the weight is the baby, placenta and amniotic fluid. Following the delivery, you still have an excess of fat to get rid of over the next couple of months.

The days and months following delivery can be very trying. Handling a newborn along with the hormonal shifts is sometimes overwhelming. Including rigorous exercise at this time is not conceivable for many women. Easing back into working out, however, helps get your energy and mood levels back on an even keel. Strength training is more important now than ever before. The body has undergone several changes that cause some amount of misalignment of muscles and joints. The arching of the lower back, the weight of the breasts and the position of breast feeding, often cause the shoulder to roll forward, stretching the muscles of the upper back, causing pain. Specific strengthening of the upper back and chest muscles is necessary. Similarly, working on the abdominal and lower back muscles will not only tighten the stretched abdominal wall but also prevent back pain. Strengthening the arms and legs help with daily tasks like carrying the baby, squatting and lifting.

The objective of weight training in the post-delivery months is to strengthen the core, align the spine and prevent pain. Weight training also revs up the metabolism to help you burn the pregnancy fat. It builds a stronger body to help you cope with the new responsibilities. You can choose to train either with external weights like dumb-bells or use your own body weight to perform many of the exercises. Strength training twice a week is sufficient in the post-delivery months. Include walking or any other aerobic activity of your choice at least three days a week along with stretches, yoga, breathing and meditation.

Following a normal delivery, one can get back to exercising as soon as one is comfortable. Most of my patients begin their abdominal and back exercises on the third or fourth day after delivery and gradually build up intensity, add weight training within the next ten days and start their cardio as early as possible.

Following a caesarean, one will need to wait six weeks or after their first post-natal check-up to start working out. They can, however, begin breathing exercises to gain control of the abdominal muscles at the earliest. Stretching, walking around and getting back to being mobile as early as possible is advised. The days in which women lay around in bed for the first couple of months following their delivery are long gone.

MENOPAUSE AND POST MENOPAUSE

Weight/strength training and flexibility are perhaps the most important aspects of fitness during menopause and in the post-menopausal years.

Building strong muscles against resistance also protects the bones against osteoporosis and fractures, so common in older women.

One of the main reasons for infirmity in older women is not because they cannot run an eight-minute mile but because they are not strong enough to handle their own bodies and daily tasks. Stronger, healthier muscles keep them standing tall, both literally and figuratively. What I see among older Indian women is either frail bodies with very little muscle mass or large women with very little muscle mass and plenty of fat. A strong, well-muscled older woman would be hard to find.

Older women are easier to train, however. By the time you reach your forties, fifties and sixties, you have de-focused from physical appearance alone and are now concentrating on staying healthy. Fitness and not weight is the priority. Not surprisingly, the benefit of this approach is a better-quality body.

By and large, older women are more sensible, dedicated and less inclined to experiment with the endless loop of yo-yo dieting and/or binge eating. They seem to have their priorities finally determined and probably also have more time to focus on themselves.

Recap

- Strength training can begin as early as eight to nine years of age using own-body-weight exercises.
- Young girls especially need to be taught that physical strength is an important aspect of health and wellness.
- Weight training is not contraindicated in pregnancy. Strengthening certain muscles that tend to be weak or over stretched will circumvent many of the physical problems during pregnancy. It should however preferably be done under proper guidance.
- Post- delivery – Strength is extremely helpful while

getting back in shape and preventing the postural problems commonly seen while breast feeding.
- Strength training is absolutely essential through menopause and after to prevent osteoporosis and build strength to maintain independence and functionality.

15

BASIC WEIGHT-TRAINING EXERCISES

Every Woman's Needs

In this chapter I will give you eleven weight-training exercises that are essential to build muscle. There are hundreds more. There are several variations of the ones described. Learning these basics will be a great place to start weight training.

Body Part	Name of Exercise	Sets and Repetitions
Chest	Bench press	3 sets, 8-12 repetitions
	Push-ups	3 sets, 10-20 repetitions
Back	Bent-over rowing	3 sets, 8-12 repetitions
Shoulders	Shoulder press	3 sets, 8-12 repetitions
Glutes	Squats without	3 sets, 25-30 repetitions
and thighs	weights	3 sets, 10-12 repetitions
(hamstrings	Squats with	3 sets, 10-20 repetitions
and quads)	weights	each leg
	Lunges	

Glutes, hamstrings and lower back	Bent-knee dead lift	3 sets, 8-12 repetitions
Glutes, hamstrings, lower back, core and shoulders	Clean and press	3 sets, 8-12 repetitions
Arms	Bicep curls	3 sets, 8-12 repetitions
	Tricep extensions	3 sets, 8-12 repetitions
Calves	Calf raises	3 sets, 25 repetitions

An illustration representing the starting position and the final position demonstrates each exercise. Please remember, as a beginner it is important to initially work under a qualified instructor who can recognize and correct your mistakes. It's hard for a beginner to understand the perfect 'form of exercise' from pictures and illustrations.

Do three to four sets of each exercise. Each set consists of eight to twelve repetitions. Rest for about thirty seconds between sets. The entire routine can be repeated two to three times a week for improvement in muscle strength and size.

1. BENCH PRESS

The bench press is an alternative to the push-up. You could start with the bench press and increase in strength in your chest and tricep muscles by gradually increasing the weight you use and then proceed to do the push-ups.

Many women can barely do the chest press properly with 2-kg weights to begin with, so I would imagine it would be very difficult for them to do a proper push-up. Build up to benching at least 10 to 12 kg and you will find the push-up becomes much easier.

Starting Position – Lie flat on a bench holding the dumbbells in your hands, palms facing towards the feet, elbows bent at ninety degrees at shoulder level.

Action – Extend the elbows such that the dumb-bells are held directly above the shoulders, the arms parallel to each other. Bring them back to starting position.

Repeat eight to twelve time and do three to four sets with thirty seconds' rest between sets.

The same exercise can be done with a barbell and plates.

Breathing – Exhale as your push the dumbbell upward and inhale as you lower the hand.

Muscles Worked – Pectoralis major and minor (or the pecs – chest muscles), anterior deltoid or the front of the shoulders and triceps.

Mistakes to Avoid

» Avoid holding your breath at any cost.
» The arms should be at shoulder level when bent (starting position).
» Avoid dropping the elbows too far below the bench at the end of each repetition. This tends to put an enormous strain on the joint.
» Bring the arms almost parallel to each other at the end of the lift holding them directly above the shoulders. Avoid flaying the arms to the side with the weights. If that happens, the weight you are lifting is clearly too heavy for you to handle.

» If the lower back arches too much, you could place your feet on edge of the bench to flatten the back.

» Getting up from the lying-down position with the weights is tricky. If you have a spotter (perhaps your trainer), she could take the weights away from you (especially if they are heavy), before you get up off the bench. If you do not have a spotter, then hold the weight close to the torso and rise up, alternately place the weights on the ground as close to the bench as possible before standing up.

2. PUSH-UP

The push-up is considered a key exercise to strengthen the upper body. It uses no equipment and is easily learnt. It uses one's own body weight and helps one understand how to handle that weight, while engaging the entire body.

If you cannot do a push-up properly, you need to either increase the strength of your upper body or lose enough weight from your body so it can be 'pushed up' by the arms and chest.

I have described the advanced push-up. In the beginner

and intermediate versions, the knees remain on the ground to reduce degree of difficulty.

Starting Position – On your hands and toes. The hands are placed below the shoulders and are placed slightly wider than the shoulders.

Action – Bend the elbows outward and slightly backward as you lower the upper body down towards the floor. Lower yourself until the chest almost touches the floor between your hands. Extend the elbows and straighten up to starting position. Perform ten to twenty repetitions and do three to four sets.

Rest for thirty seconds between sets.

Breathing – Inhale as you lower. Exhale as you straighten up.

Muscles Worked – Pectoralis major and minor (or the pecs – chest muscles), triceps, anterior deltoid or the front of the shoulder and the core muscles.

Care must be taken to see that the back is flat and abs are tight and engaged throughout the exercise.

The position on the toes is the advanced push-up. In the **beginner version,** the knees are placed on the ground directly below the hips and the identical action of lowering the upper body is performed. In the **intermediate push-up,** the knees are still on the ground but moved further back behind the hips so the degree of difficulty is increased. In all the versions, the back remains flat through the exercise.

Mistakes to Avoid

» The position of the hands remain below the shoulders. Therefore, when the body is lowered, the face should almost touch down **in front of the hands, not between**

them and the chest should almost touch down between the hands.

» Keep the back absolutely flat and abs engaged, whether you are doing the beginners', intermediate or advanced version of the exercise.

» Keep the head down and the cervical spine aligned.

3. BENT-OVER ROWING

Bent-over rowing works the upper back muscles. The back is rarely worked in daily life. Any pulling action of the arms will work the back.

Starting Position – Bend over by hinging at the hip joint. Bend the knees slightly, keeping them soft. The upper body should be almost parallel to the ground. Hold the dumb-bells in your hands, hanging down directly below the shoulders, palms facing each other.

Action – Breath out and pull back in a rowing action, bending the elbows until the dumb-bells are almost at the waist level. Squeeze the shoulder blades in this position. Lower to starting position.

Do eight to twelve repetitions and three sets. Rest for thirty seconds between sets.

Breathing – Exhale as you pull back, inhale as you lower the weight.

Muscles Worked – Latissimus dorsi (the large back muscles), rhomboids (the muscles between the shoulder blades), part of the trapezius (the neck muscles) and the biceps.

Mistakes to Avoid

» Keep the back absolutely flat and head up through the entire exercise. Often we see clients with a curled spine attempting to perform this exercise. That spells disaster.
» Keep the knees slightly bent and soft. Straightening the knees puts a strain on the lower back.
» While bending the elbows, keep them as close to the torso as possible and avoid bending them outwards.

4. SHOULDER PRESS

Starting Position – Sit with the back erect. Hold the dumb-bells with palms facing forward, and the arms bent at ninety degrees at shoulder level, as shown in the illustration.

Action – Extend the elbows and lift the weight overhead bringing the arms together so they are parallel to one another (but not touching). Hold for a few seconds and lower to starting position.

Do three sets and eight to twelve repetitions in each set. Rest for thirty seconds between sets.

Breathing – Exhale as you lift the weight. Inhale as you lower.

Muscle Worked – The entire deltoid or shoulder muscle.

Once again, there are several variations of this exercise. As you advance, you could use the barbell instead of the dumbbell.

Mistakes to Avoid

» As you lift your arms overhead, avoid dropping them too wide as that puts an enormous strain on the joint itself.

» The chest needs to be open and the whole action is carried out in the vertical plane adjacent to the ears. Often, we see clients lifting the weight almost in front of the face and pushing forwards instead of upward. You could initially use the shoulder-press machine to avoid this mistake.

5. THE SQUAT

Starting Position—Stand with feet hip-width apart. Hands may be placed on the hips, out in front of you or crossed across your chest.

Action—Sit back (like you would sit in a chair), hinging first at the hip joint, lowering the hips almost down to the level of the knees. Don't allow the knees to travel beyond your toes. Stand up by extending the hips and knees.

Do three sets. Number of repetitions can be increased up to twenty-five to thirty when the exercise is done without weights. When weights are added, the repetitions will decrease.

Muscles Worked—Quadriceps, glutes and hamstrings.

Breathing—Inhale as you lower and exhale as you straighten up.

There are numerous variations of the squat. Positioning the feet differently addresses slightly different areas of the same muscles to varying degrees. Adding weights, either dumb-bells or a barbell across the shoulders, adds intensity to build muscle.

The wide squat, where the feet are placed wide and toes point outward while you squat in the centre, brings the inner thighs into play.

The hack squat uses the hack squat machine, allowing you to lift very heavy weights.

The squat is a very powerful exercise. It uses the largest muscles in the body—the glutes, quads and hamstrings. Doing squats, especially in rapid succession, will cause some breathlessness and increase in heart rate as a result of such large muscles having come into play. A squat workout can even be used as a form of cardio.

Squats form one of the foundation exercises of the weight-training armamentarium, building strong thighs that help to stabilize and protect the knees. Conversely, doing squats incorrectly can actually cause damage and injury to the knees.

Mistakes to Avoid

» While squatting, the knees should ideally remain behind the position of the toes. While squatting wide, the knees should not travel inward. Tall women, however, with long legs may find this difficult to manage. A certain amount of 'knees travelling in front of the feet' is acceptable for long-limbed individuals as long as the major weight of the upper body is on the glutes and thighs.

» The torso leans too far forward while squatting. Many women try to compensate for inadequate leg strength by bending forward while squatting. The upper body needs to be erect and upright even as you lower by bending at the hips and knees.

» While doing wide squats, avoid having the knees roll inward as you squat. They should remain over the respective ankles.

» Learning how to do the squat properly is the best thing you can do to get those sculpted legs and glutes.

Having learnt to do the basic narrow and wide squats you can progress to using weights, adding jump squats, sumo squats, pulse squats and one-legged squats, among other variations to challenge yourself.

6. THE LUNGE

The lunge is a form of a squat as it uses the major leg muscles. It is a dynamic exercise, as you have to move by constantly stepping forward and back. It is a real fun exercise once you learn how to do it properly.

Starting Position—Stand erect holding the dumb-bells in both hands. Hands hang down by the sides.

Action—Step forward with the right foot and bend the right knee so that the right thigh is almost parallel to the ground. Make sure the right knee does not go beyond the right foot. The left leg will be extended behind you, knee extended and heel raised.

Step back to staring position and repeat the action with the left foot stepping forward.

Do about ten to twenty repetitions on each leg. Rest for thirty seconds and do two more sets.

Breathing – Inhale as you step forward and exhale as you step back.

Muscles Worked—Quadriceps, glutes, hamstrings and the core.

The lunge is different from the squat mainly due to the positioning of the legs. The weight of the body is primarily on the front leg that is bent at the knee.

Mistakes to Avoid

» Care should be taken not to allow the front knee to travel beyond the toes when the knee bends.
» The upper body remains upright and head held high.
» Arms hang down beside the upper body.
» Abs remain tight.

There are numerous variations of the lunge, starting with the basic alternating forward lunge. One can move on to pulse lunges, Bulgarian split squat (which is actually a lunge, with the back foot on a higher surface like a chair or stepper), back lunges and running lunges, among other variations.

7. BENT-KNEE DEAD LIFT

The Romanian dead lift is a great exercise for the hamstrings and glutes. The squat and lunge focus mainly on the quads while the dead lift is *the* exercise for the glutes, hamstrings and the lower back.

While the exercise may look like the squat it is very different.

Starting Position – Stand holding the barbell (or a pair of dumb-bells) in front of you at the level of your thighs.

Palms face your body.

Action – Start bending forward by pushing the hips back (hinging at the hip joint). In this exercise, the hip hinge is the primary movement as the upper body bends forward with the weight in the hands. The knees bend later in order to keep the barbell as close to the body as possible as it slides down the thighs. Depending on your hamstring flexibility, you may be able to go all the way down to almost touch the ground with the weight, or you may be able to only bend partly while keeping the back flat. The glutes and hamstrings work to lift the upper body and the weight up, again producing a powerful challenge.

Do three sets of eight to twelve repetitions per set.

The key is to keep the back flat. Curling the spine puts pressure on the back, and the hamstrings and glutes are removed from the equation. This is a recipe for disaster and many back injuries result from poor form of the dead lift (both the stiff-leg variety and the bent-knee dead lift)

Breathing – Inhale as you lower, exhale as you lift and straighten.

Muscles Worked – Gluteus maximus, hamstrings, erector spinae (back muscles).

Mistakes to Avoid

» Keep the back flat throughout the exercise.
» The primary movement is the hip hinge, not the bending of the knees.
» Keep the weight close to the thighs, almost running down their length.
» Keep the head up and chest lifted.

8. CLEAN AND PRESS

This is a very intense, total-body exercise. It is also an advanced exercise and a combination of the bent knee dead lift and the shoulder press. It begins with picking up a weight (dumb-bells or a barbell) from the floor, lifting it up towards the shoulders and then heaving it overhead like a shoulder press.

Starting Position – Stand before the barbell that is placed on the floor in front of you.

Action – Hinge at the hip joint, push the hips backward and bend forward, keeping the back flat, looking forward. Reach for the barbell with palms facing your body. In order to do this, you will also have to start bending the knees at some point of bending over, but make sure they don't travel beyond the toes. Pick up the barbell and lift it to thigh level.

The first half of the exercise is almost like the bent-knee dead lift.

Now rotate the arms and lift the weight towards shoulder level. From this position, lift the weight upward like a shoulder press, keeping the core engaged and taking care not to arch the back.

This exercise works almost the entire body.

Reverse the sequence of events by lowering the weight to shoulder level as in a shoulder press, rotate the hands and bring the weight down to thigh level, now hinge at the hip, pushing backward, bending slightly at the knees to lower the weight like a bent-knee dead lift.

Without placing the weight on the floor, move on to the next repetition.

Do eight to twelve repetitions and three sets. Rest for about thirty to forty seconds between sets.

Breathing — As there are multiple movements in this exercise you will need to usually take two breaths. Exhaling as you lift the barbell from the ground to straighten the body, inhaling in that position and then exhaling again as you rotate the arms and lift the weight overhead.

Muscles Worked — All the muscles worked in the bent a knee dead lift and the shoulder press are worked in this exercise.

Mistakes to Avoid

» All the mistakes to be avoided in the shoulder press and bent-knee dead lift have to be avoided here.

» As it is a combination exercise, addressing almost the entire body, it can be very taxing. Do just six to eight repetitions at first if you can and then move forward.
» Ensure every part of the exercise is perfect.
» While rotating the shoulders to move from the bent-knee dead lift to the shoulder press, make sure the weight stays as close to the body as possible.
» Some people tend to step forward with one foot for better balance while lifting overhead for the shoulder press and then stepping back when they move to complete the bent-knee dead lift. This is acceptable for better balance. Advanced exercisers, using very heavy weights, tend do this. They inherently know how to move while holding on to a weight.

As a beginner, stay with a lower weight that you can handle easily until you can perfect the sequence of the exercise.

9. BICEP CURLS

Starting Position – Stand in a comfortable stance, feet hip- width apart and knees soft. Hold the dumb-bells in your hands, palms facing forward.

Action – Curl the forearm towards the upper arm and bring the weight up to shoulder level. The action should be completed with the bicep muscle alone and not with the shoulders. Hold for two to three seconds and lower to starting position.

Do eight to twelve repetitions and three sets, resting for thirty seconds between sets.

Muscles Worked – Biceps, located at the front of the arms.

Breathing – Exhale as you curl, inhale as you lower.

Mistakes to Avoid

» The movement happens at the elbow joint. The elbows stay close to the waist and slightly in front of the plane of the body. Bend the elbow and curl the forearm until it almost reaches the shoulder level.

» When the weight is too heavy the shoulders also tend to contract, lifting the entire upper arm forward as well. The elbow will then move away from the waist. This is to be avoided if you want to focus on training the biceps.

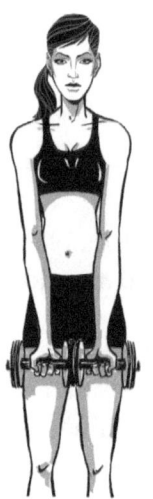 

10. OVERHEAD TRICEP EXTENSIONS

Starting Position – Stand in a comfortable stance, feet hip- width apart, holding the top of one dumbbell in both hands, palms facing upward.

Action – Extend the elbows and lift the dumbbell upward by contracting the triceps muscle. Hold for a few seconds and lower. Elbows remain close to the ears.

Do three sets, eight to twelve repetitions per set.

Breathing – Exhale as you lift, inhale as you lower.

Muscles Worked – Triceps.

Mistakes to Avoid

» Keep the elbows as close to the ears as possible.
» Keep the core engaged and avoid arching the back.
» Keep the knees soft.

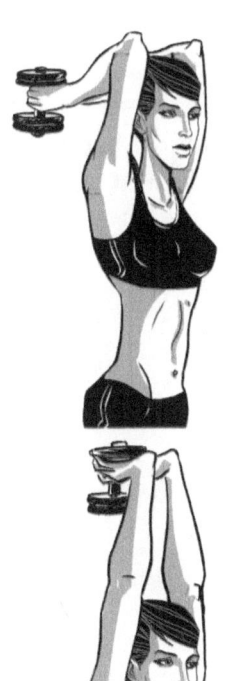

As always, there are several variations of this exercise. You could evolve to doing it by lifting the dumbbell with one arm (thereby increasing degree of difficulty) while supporting that arm. You could do it with a barbell while lying on a bench and so on.

11. CALF RAISES

Starting Position – Holding a dumbbell in each hand, stand erect either on the floor or on the edge of a very stable stepper (with the heels beyond the edge of the step).

Action – Squeeze the calves and lift your heels as high as you can off the ground to go up on your toes. Then lower the heels to below step level if you are on a stepper or to just before touching the floor if you are on the floor.

Repeat the movement fifteen to twenty-five times per set for three sets. Rest for twenty seconds between sets.

Muscles Worked – Gastrocnemius, soleus (calves).

You will be surprised at how easy it is to actually learn these exercises using a very light weight. Once you master the technique and the breathing (which is critical), you can start to increase the weight you use for each exercise. This will differ between exercises. Larger muscles like the chest, back and shoulders will be able to handle more weight while the biceps, triceps and calves can only handle less.

Only you can determine how much weight you use for each exercise.

Use a weight with which you can do about eight to twelve repetitions. The last few repetitions should be difficult. I mean, by the time you reach repetition ten, you should want to put the weight down. Then you push through the last two repetitions with sheer determination. If you are easily swinging a little dumbbell with which you can perhaps do twelve repetitions and then a dozen more, then clearly the weight is too light for you. If you want to see results, increase the weight.

FEEL THE BURN

There will come a time during the course of the set when you reach about repetition ten and the muscle begins to burn. I mean really burn, almost like the muscle is on fire. It sounds scary, but really it is not.

This is caused by the accumulation of lactic acid (a metabolic by-product of the energy cycle providing the fuel for the muscles to work). The lactic acid cannot be removed from the working muscle fast enough as you do repetition after repetition. The oxygen supply and the removal of waste from the working muscle cannot keep up with the exercise and the production of the waste. So, it builds up within the muscle, causing the burn. Finally you stop the set after ten or twelve repetitions and the blood flowing through the muscles washes lactic acid away, causing relief.

This happens almost instantaneously and you find you can do another set with a rest of about twenty to thirty seconds.

If you are using very heavy weights, however, you will be able to complete only about six to eight repetitions and the rest between sets will need to be about a minute.

This feeling can be quite intimidating for the beginner. A thoughtful instructor will always explain what happens during the workout and why it happens in order to enlighten exercisers. After a couple of sessions, one gets used to the sensation and understands implicitly how to handle it and how hard to push.

'Feel the burn' has often been used as a catchy fitness phrase in forms of advertising. I believe sometimes students pushed beyond their limits especially in forms like crossfit or rigorous boot camp.

'No pain, no gain', 'impossible is nothing' and many such attractive slogans are taken to an art form.

Is that really necessary?

As I have mentioned before, the human body adapts and it surely will, but in the meantime, it may be wise to avoid injury as well. Training requires technique and the ability to ease the body slowly into a routine and then push just enough to see improvement. Pushing too much can end with more trouble than progress.

I did mention that the human body is quite remarkable, but push it recklessly and it is sure to rebel!

Recap

- In this chapter I have explained the 'form' (or method of doing) some basic weight training exercises.
- There are of course hundreds of other exercises

addressing the same muscles, which I hope you will gradually want to learn once you start enjoying weight training.

- Each of the exercises has to be done in a specific way with a particular breathing pattern. This is critical to prevent injury.
- The weight used for each exercise will vary depending on the strength of the muscles being trained.
- The number of repetitions and sets of each exercise can vary, but initially you could do three sets of ten to twelve repetitions for each exercise.
- By the end of every set, you should 'feel the burn' in your working muscles, indicating that they are being challenged.

*Illustrations in this chapter by Mohit Suneja

16

CARDIO

EPOC, REE and HIIT—Getting the Best Out of
Your Cardiovascular Exercises

Now that we know the basics of weight training, we need to understand our cardiovascular exercise options. While weight training increases and strengthen the skeletal muscles, cardiovascular exercises strengthens the heart, lungs and the circulatory system. Any activity that increases ones heart rate can be categorized as cardio. You can choose your favourite, be it running, speed walking, step class, kickboxing, or any other available options.

Remember that the class is only as good as the instructor. If you have an instructor who is well trained and knowledgeable about body mechanics, she will be able to watch out for potential injury and offer various low-impact and simpler options for the same moves in the class. She should also be very aware of her student's fitness levels and understand who is capable of what. She should be able to make the class interesting and challenging for all the fitness levels.

The key is to get the heart rate up and keep it elevated

for at least twenty to forty minutes (not necessarily continuously).

In order to get the best out of your cardio workout, you need to use strategies to work smarter, not longer. EPOC and REE are factors to figure while training smart.

EPOC AND REE

Two fancy terms often thrown around in fitness circles.

EPOC stands for Excess Post-exercise Oxygen Consumption and REE stands for Resting Energy Expenditure.

Have you ever touched the bonnet of a car immediately after it has been running a while? It feels warm. The heat generated during the drive sustains for a little longer.

Similarly, after an exercise routine the body is revved up and running at a higher rate of metabolism, burning more calories than before the exercise. We all know that a bout of running causes our heart rate to speed up, body temperature to rise, we break out in a sweat, breathing becomes harder and the working muscles begin to tire and ache. After completing the session the body takes a while to return to normal homeostasis.

Return to normal homeostasis represents a variety of processes within the body:

» Replenishment of the glycogen stores within the muscles, which have been depleted during the course of the exercise.
» Restoration of lactate levels in the muscles and the blood.

» Re-oxygenation of the blood and restoration of circulating hormones.
» Lowering body temperature.
  ♦ Return of the heart rate to normal.
  ♦ Re-establishment of rate of respiration to normal.

All this requires energy and calories.

EPOC, otherwise called the **After Burn,** is essentially the excess calories that continue to be expended following an exercise session in order to achieve all the above.

Without our even recognizing it, some forms of exercise keep the body metabolism elevated much longer; in other words, they have a higher EPOC. We do not necessarily feel any different. Our body is just burning more calories even while at rest.

Is it not that the coolest thing to happen, especially if you are looking at losing fat?

Not all forms of exercise do this to our bodies, however. Following a low-intensity, long-duration session of cardio, like a long, low or moderate intensity walk, the body tends to return to normal metabolism and homeostasis quite quickly.

Following a higher-intensity cardio routine or following a heavy weight-training session, however, keeps the EPOC elevated for almost twenty-four hours. It makes sense therefore, to throw in a couple of sessions of HIIT or High-Intensity Interval Training a week and most certainly ensure that you train with weights regularly.

REE is the amount of energy the body requires to sustain daily normal activity, including the working of the heart, breathing, digestion, routine activity, and so on. It is basically the calories we burn during the course of the day.

The muscles in the body are responsible for a majority of the REE. The protein turnover (that is the muscle-protein breakdown and synthesis) within the muscles consumes enormous amounts of energy. Since most of the REE can be attributed to the muscles in the body, it stands to reason then that a more muscular body will burn more calories even while at rest. These calories, or energy to provide ATP for the protein turnover, are tapped from fat-storage depots within the body. Thus the body is using its own fat to sustain itself.

Gain more muscle and lose more fat!

HIGH-INTENSITY INTERVAL TRAINING—(HIIT) VS LOW-INTENSITY LONG-DURATION CARDIO

HIIT is the new buzz word. Gone are the days of putting in long hours of boring cardio. **Now saving time and making workouts shorter and more intense is the call of the day.**

HIIT cardio is a way of training your cardiovascular system or increasing stamina. As the name implies, short bursts of very high-intensity (sometimes all-out intensity) cardio activity are followed by a brief rest or recovery interval. This is called a **challenge-and-recovery cycle.**

The challenge will be the high-intensity segment. It could be a sprint on a track, increasing speed and/or inclining your bike while cycling or increasing the intensity on a cross-trainer. It does not matter which machine or mode of cardio you use. All you need to do is increase your intensity. If you go all-out and increase intensity to 90 to 100 per cent, the chances are that you will not be able to sustain it for longer than about ten to thirty seconds at the most. Following this challenge phase, you go into the recovery phase, which does not mean you sit down on the park bench to rest. Instead you run/walk, cycle, cross-train at a lower intensity to catch your breath. The rest phase typically ranges anywhere from ten to sixty seconds and in some routines can even be increased to four minutes.

The challenge-and-recovery cycle is repeated several times for about twenty minutes. This can be done as groups of challenge-recovery cycles where each group is called a 'set' with longer rest intervals between sets.

This form of cardio is highly demanding on the body. You push the body to its limit repeatedly over and over again. Although the total time taken is only about twenty minutes, those twenty minutes can be extremely challenging.

You can formulate your own HIIT. Start with a shorter challenge phase and build up gradually. The recovery phase should be just long enough for you to catch your breath and gather the strength to push yourself for another challenge. This kind of training is not for the faint-hearted. It is also not recommended every day of the week. When done about two to three days a week, it has been found that HIIT is very effective in burning fat; particularly the fat around the belly.

This does not mean one should do away with long-duration, lower-intensity exercise altogether. Those with lower fitness levels may not tolerate HIIT well. Besides, HIIT cannot be done every day of the week. Injuries are also more common with HIIT owing to the fact that one pushes oneself to the limit repeatedly. When the body fatigues, as it surely will, chances of injury increase.

The **TABATA** routine is a very popular form of HIIT training.

It typically advocates twenty seconds of challenge followed by only ten seconds of rest, repeated about seven to eight times. This totals only about four minutes a 'set'. Several sets can be repeated with longer rest intervals in-between.

In another protocol called the **Wingate Protocol**, the challenge phase lasts thirty seconds followed by a four-minute recovery. The cycle is repeated about six times.

You can, however, format your own HIIT challenge-recovery segments? according to your fitness level. Do it twice a week to increase the fat-burning capacity of your body and also increase your cardiovascular endurance or stamina.

BENEFITS OF HIIT OVER LONG-DURATION CARDIO

» *Increases EPOC and REE:* One of the most important benefits of HIIT is ability of the body to continue to burn fat (due to increased REE or EPOC) for more than twenty-four hours after the exercise.

» *Improves insulin sensitivity:* HIIT has also been found to improve insulin sensitivity in diabetics. This could mean that one could lower the requirement for insulin or other oral diabetic medication for the patients if they participate in HIIT two to three times a week.

» *Decreases belly fat:* Following HIIT, the increased REE or EPOC leads to an increase in fat loss, particularly abdominal fat.

» *Improves stamina:* HIIT increases stamina, making it possible for you to do more. The challenge phase defies the body to work harder than you normally would in a long-duration cardio session. The heart then has to improve to accommodate this workload, which it does, very effectively.

» *Prevents loss of muscle:* An important benefit of HIIT is that given the shorter duration of the exercise and the challenge it produces to the muscles, it prevents muscle loss, which is sometimes seen in long-duration, lower-intensity cardio. This, to me, seems like a very important benefit since my whole postulation to lose fat is to maintain and build muscle mass.

» *Can be done anywhere:* You can do HIIT anywhere. Indoors on a spin bike, treadmill or a cross-trainer, or outdoors on a track or in the park. It is, however, not easy to do HIIT on a treadmill. The machine cannot change speeds fast enough to incorporate quick changes in challenge-and-recovery cycles. All-out effort followed by immediate recovery does not translate well on a treadmill. There is a very high possibility you may fall off the back of the treadmill when it does not slow down fast enough following the challenge phase, which can be quite catastrophic. There is a way around that, however, as shown in the sample protocols below. The trick is not to change the speed too much and keep the incline on the treadmill constant.

» *Saves time:* The time saved is enormous when doing HIIT. It is a great workout when you have just half an hour to spare and want to get your cardio out of the way.

» *Improves aerobic fitness and increases lactate threshold:* HIIT improves both aerobic fitness (stamina) and anaerobic fitness. Towards the end of the challenge phase the muscles cope with minimum oxygen supply. They go into anaerobic (without oxygen) metabolism. Their ability to continue to function in this anaerobic environment is improved with consecutive HIIT routines. In other words, their 'lactate threshold' increases.

DRAWBACKS OF HIIT

» *Not suitable for beginners:* Obviously, HIIT is not for everyone. I wouldn't recommend it for someone starting out on her fitness journey.
» *Not suitable for the obese:* It can also be problematic for someone who is extremely obese. It is far better to lose much of the fat initially using a lower-intensity, longer-duration cardio workout, which is easy on the joints. Once you have improved in fitness levels and lost weight, you can start HIIT.
» *Requires self-motivation:* HIIT requires a great deal of motivation. The challenge phase can cause considerable discomfort for those not used to pushing their body beyond the limit and may be discouraging.
» *Can predispose to injury:* One is more prone to injury, especially if fitness levels are poor or if one does HIIT too often.

SOME HIIT ROUTINES

» *Sprint training* (can be done on a track)
  • Warm up for seven to ten minutes with light jogging or brisk walking.
  • Sprint for twenty seconds – Challenge phase.

* Jog or walk for ten seconds — Recovery phase.
* The Challenge:Recovery ratio is 2:1 in this format.

Repeat the challenge-recovery cycles ten times, depending on your fitness level. Each cycle lasts 30 seconds. The entire 'set' of ten to fifteen cycles will take you about five minutes in total.

Rest for two minutes by walking slower.

Then repeat the above set two more times if possible. The total time for the workout will be about twenty-one minutes.

Cool down for another five to seven minutes.

» *Treadmill workout*
* Warm up for seven to ten minutes with light jogging. Put the treadmill on an incline of between five to fifteen, depending on your fitness level.
* Increase the speed on the treadmill and run at about 5 to 7 miles per hour for a minute (or you can start with running for thirty seconds). This is the Challenge phase.
* Decrease the speed (leave the incline constant through the workout) and walk for two minutes. This is the Recovery phase.
* The Challenge:Recovery ratio is 2:1 in this format.

Repeat the challenge-recovery cycles six to seven times.

If the challenge phase is difficult to keep up with, you can reduce the time of the challenge and recovery to begin with, keeping the ratio as 1:2.

The total time taken for this format will be between eighteen to twenty minutes.

Cool down for five to seven minutes.

Alternately, you can introduce various exercises into your challenge and recovery instead of using running/walking in your HIIT.

Warm up for about seven minutes.

Activity	Time
Push-ups	40 seconds
Rest	20 seconds
Jump squats	40 seconds
Rest	20 seconds
Plank with alternate knee to elbow	40 seconds
Rest	20 seconds
Side shuffles	40 seconds
Rest	20 seconds
Alternate lunges or running lunges	40 seconds
Rest	20 seconds
Burpees	40 seconds
Rest	20 seconds
Sprint in place	40 seconds
Rest	20 seconds
Jumping Jacks	40 seconds
Rest	20 seconds
Plank and twist	40 seconds
Rest	20 seconds
Wide pulse squat	40 seconds
Rest	20 seconds

The whole cycle will last 10 minutes. Repeat the cycle two time for a total of twenty minutes.

Similarly, you can format your own challenge and

recovery cycles. The ratios of the challenge and recovery need to be kept constant through the entire workout. A couple of sessions of HIIT a week can work wonders for fat loss.

LOW-INTENSITY, LONG-DURATION CARDIO

Lower-intensity, longer-duration exercise has the advantage of being less stressful to the body and creates less chance of injury. It could prove to be much more manageable and fun, especially for those who are not fit and just starting out on their fitness journey.

We have all heard the fitness claims that lower-intensity, longer-duration cardio causes the body to get into a 'fat-burning zone'. This is true, in the sense that when working out at a lower intensity, a larger percentage of energy required for the workout comes from fat, given the fact that oxygen is readily available for use by the muscles at the lower intensity. In a higher-intensity workout the muscles tend to use glucose as a source of energy as fat oxidation takes far too long to accommodate this level of intensity.

However, one must understand that the total number of calories burnt is what eventually determines fat loss over time. HIIT tends to burn a larger number of overall calories due to higher amounts of overall energy expenditure.

Besides, the total overall number of calories being greater, HIIT creates a higher 'after burn' or EPOC as already discussed, making you more efficient at continuing to burn extra calories through the day.

I love longer-duration, moderate-intensity cardio and would never do away with it altogether. It acts as a stress reliever more than anything else! A long walk or bike ride or a moderate-intensity class of aerobics are all fun and keep the calorie ledger ringing.

THE MARATHON

A marathon is an extreme version of the long-duration, low-intensity exercise. The 42 km requires not only stamina and muscle endurance but a huge measure of mental fortitude as well. I think it takes a certain kind of temperament, training and investment of time and energy.

There has in the recent past been a surge of enthusiasm in marathon running in the major cities across our country. Popularized by celebrities, it seems rather fashionable to claim to have 'run a marathon' (although most people run/walk most of the way). Almost a rite of passage, one might say. While I think it is wonderful that the marathon is getting so much attention and encouraging more women to get out there, there is a huge lacuna in training and continuity with exercise for most women. There is also negligence towards building muscle, to protect the joints of the lower body from the assault they endure during the long runs and training sessions.

One also wonders how many of these thousands of women who participate in the event when it is held once a year actually exercise the rest of the year.

Women face specific problems while running, like an increase in the Q angle, causing more stress on the knee joint, and the larger fat percentage (than some men at least) leading to a greater strain being placed on the knees. These problems can be managed and circumvented with the proper training. I am not certain, though, that women are getting such training consistently.

> I was asked to talk at a pre-marathon session in Mumbai in 2014. I was also asked to run the marathon because I was 'fit'. Being 'fit' does not necessarily mean one can run a marathon.
>
> I simply had no desire to run a marathon and have never had. I love running, but only short distances. On the treadmill or track, I usually run about 5 to 7 km. So I ended up just talking to the participants pre-marathon, along with the other panellists, the beautiful Gul Panag and truly inspiring Roshini Bakshi.
>
> The only time I think I have run over 15 km was when I got lost on my run in Chicago and ran around in circles (slightly panicked, I might add) trying to find my way back home. I did not have Google Maps and my sense of direction is appalling. Not the ideal combination to go running alone in a new city, I agree...
>
> Still the positive take on that incident is that I now know I can run at least 15 km if I am forced to!

Not everyone can be a marathon runner. If you want to be one, you need to train regularly and work towards running the marathon. You cannot wake up one fine morning and decide to attempt one. It takes a different kind of training, nutrition and attitude. It is also more about the spirit than the body. As with anything that needs to be enduring, one has to have the right mental attitude to sustain the energy required to see it through.

One has to be careful not to overtrain which is a very real possibility when trying to lose fat. One has to also consider nutrient intake. If not nourished properly, the body will not respond and the likelihood of fatigue, overtraining and prospect of injury increases.

In general, aerobic exercise makes you a better 'fat burner'. Resistance or weight training adds to the body's ability to burn fat by the increase in muscle. So the combination of cardio and weight training is important in fat loss.

Recap

- There are various forms of cardio to challenge your heart and lungs (cardiovascular system).
- EPOC or Excess Post-exercise Oxygen Consumption is the excess energy that continues to be burnt after certain forms of exercise. EPOC is typically more after a high intensity workout or after weight training. It is otherwise called the 'afterburn'.
- REE or Resting Energy Expenditure is the amount of energy required to sustain normal daily activity and existence.
- REE is more when the body is carrying more muscle.
- In other words—Building more muscle will burn more calories (and therefore fat).
- HIIT or High Intensity Interval Training is a form of cardio that is very short in duration and brilliant at burning more fat. There are different protocols you could follow. It also has a high EPOC.
- Low intensity, long duration cardio on the other hand does not continue to burn calories like HIIT does.

17

REST AND RECOVERY

Results Require Rest and Recovery

Rest and recovery are as important as exercise itself. Muscles repair themselves and grow in the rest phase between two weight-training sessions. Not resting enough between sessions could be the biggest deterrent to muscle growth. Excessive cardio, especially at very high intensity without adequate rest can cause more damage than progress. One of the other big problems with too much cardio is loss of muscle mass.

SLEEP

Sleep is the healer of all things. Your body is completely rested and this is the only time the brain is not besieged with relentless external stimuli. Most people require six to eight hours of uninterrupted sleep a night. Athletes require more. From a weight-loss perspective, long-term sleep deprivation has been found to cause weight gain. It is even implicated in metabolic syndrome, diabetes and hypertension, all of which affect your weight.

The two hormones responsible for weight gain may be leptin and ghrelin. Ghrelin is the hormone that causes hunger and increases appetite. Ghrelin increases with sleep deprivation. Leptin, on the other hand, which is the satiety hormone, decreases with lack of sleep. A combination of the two hormones causes hunger and overeating. There is a leaning especially towards the wrong food. Consequently, weight gain ensues.

Insulin has also been found to be responsible for some of the problems associated with sleep deprivation or even disturbed sleep rhythms as seen in people who work night shifts, like doctors and nurses.

Lack of sleep and the consequent fatigue prevents you from making sensible choices. This includes food choices. The chances of indulgence and binging on the wrong foods are more common. A tired mind and body are always looking for some kind of a pick-me-up, which could be in the form of food, cigarettes, alcohol or caffeine. The mind is also unable to figure out the difference between fatigue and hunger. Thus we reach for food.

Lack of sleep naturally causes fatigue and a resulting decrease in physical activity during the day. It is hard to imagine trying to get to a gym when one is exhausted and sleep deprived. You will most likely also try to decrease daily physical activity, sit around more, nap, feel drowsy and generally have below-par productivity.

Eating late at night, especially a high-carbohydrate meal, can shorten sleep and affect weight. Insulin has a circadian rhythm and is least effective at night. Eating late into the night makes it more difficult for the body to metabolize sugars.

Sleep is also a healer of muscles. Inadequate sleep prevents muscle healing. **The muscles heal and grow between sessions of exercise (not during)**. Not only is it important to get at least a gap of forty-eight hours between training the same group of muscles, but it is also important to get enough sleep during that time. If you are working round the clock and go back into the gym, even if it is after forty-eight hours, your training and muscle growth will suffer. Your muscles require rest and recuperation.

There are ways to ensure better sleep. The Internet too, abounds with all kinds of advice regarding how to get enough sleep. Alcohol must be consumed in limited amounts for it disturbs sleep; keep the room you sleep in dark, quiet and cool; stay away from the television and the computer and have a nightly routine. Suffice is to say you have to find your own routine. Sleep is important. Period. Respect it. Value it and do not compromise on it.

HYDRATION

Another important prerequisite to healthy muscles, effective workouts and growth is proper hydration. Adequate fluid replacement helps to maintain hydration during exercise. It is also important to prevent dehydration and heatstrokes, and improve performance.

The American College of Sports Medicine recommends that one drink about 500 millilitre of water about two hours before exercise and sips of water throughout the workout session. It is also advised that the fluid consumed be cool in order to lower body temperature. In an exercise session lasting about an hour, good old water should be sufficient to rehydrate you, as the body is more than capable of supplying the energy needed for that hour.

Aside from the fluid intake during an exercise session, continuing to hydrate through the day is essential. In colder weather one has to sometimes make a conscious effort to drink water. Since water makes up 60 per cent of the human body it is easy to see why it is so important. Water is necessary to carry out normal functions in the body, flush out toxins and carry nutrients to your cells, among a plethora of other activities.

The general recommendation of, 'drink eight, eight-ounce glasses of water a day', is commonly remembered. However, this changes with various other factors.

» Exercise obviously will call for a greater intake (aside from the eight, eight-ounce glasses per day).
» The higher the intensity of the exercise the more you are likely to sweat, which means you will need to top up with more water.
» The same applies when the duration of the exercise is longer than an hour.
» In hot, humid weather it is essential that one drinks more. Indoor heating can cause moisture loss from the skin.
» Higher altitudes trigger increase in urination and breathing that may, in turn, call for an increase in water intake.

Sipping with a straw has been found to increase the intake of water! Similarly, flavouring the water with a slice of lemon will encourage drinking.

How do you know you are drinking enough water?

» You are not thirsty.
» Your urine is clear and plenty.
» Your skin looks plump and healthy.
» You feel good and energetic.
» You have normal bowel movements.

Symptoms like headache, irritability, dry mouth, sunken eyes, dry skin and constipation are indicative of dehydration.

WATER INTOXICATION

There is such a thing as drinking too much water too.

When this happens the kidneys may not be able to excrete the excess water and this causes dilution of the electrolytes in the blood and a condition called 'hyponatremia' or low sodium levels.

Symptoms of hyponatremia:

» Nausea and vomiting
» Headache and confusion
» Loss of energy, restlessness, irritability
» Even seizures and coma, when extreme

NUTRITION

Fitness and nutrition go hand in hand. It is impossible to be fit if you are not properly nourished. This is one of the reasons why very-low-calorie diets that deprive you of entire food groups do not support exercise. The body cannot cope with trying to work out without enough fuel. Such diets also cause muscle loss, something one must vigilantly guard oneself against.

A well-balanced diet that includes all the food groups in the proper proportions is essential for a healthy body.

FAT LOSS OR MUSCLE GAIN?

How then, does one go about losing fat and retaining and building muscle?

The truth is, losing fat and building muscle require completely contrasting calorific intakes. Fat loss requires a diet that is slightly calorie deficient whereas muscle building requires a diet that is slightly in excess of requirement.

It is difficult to do both, lose fat and build muscle effectively and simultaneously. It can, however, be done in phases.

Someone who is obese will need to initially go on the calorie-deficient diet to lose fat. Training with weights at the same time will ensure that muscle is not lost while on such a diet. Over a period of time, the body begins to lose fat and gain muscle. Calorie adjustments need to be made continuously to keep pace with the body's requirements.

Gaining muscle will increase the basal metabolic rate or BMR of the body and subsequently the calorie requirement as well. Eventually, the objective should be to enable us to eat well, nourish the body and continue to exercise.

CREATING A FAT-LOSS DIET

To create a fat-loss diet, you will first have to determine how many calories you are currently consuming. Write down every single thing you eat in a day for a whole week and evaluate your approximate calorie intake per day. From that value subtract 300 to 500 calories per day to lose fat. Losing about half a kilogram a week is a healthy objective.

Establish your protein intake first. It needs to be about a gram/kilogram of your body weight. Protein provides 4 calories/gram.

After introducing protein, divide the rest of your calories available between carbohydrates and fats. Ensure you consume complex carbohydratess like fruits, vegetables and whole grains from the carbohydrates group. Fats should be mainly from unrefined oils like olive, sesame, peanut, coconut and soy, and from foods like avocado, nuts, seeds and oily fish.

STRETCHING

Flexibility is the fourth pillar of fitness.

Flexibility is extremely important, but highly underestimated. As we age, our muscles tend to get less flexible or elastic leading to aches, pains and decreased mobility. Stretching regularly is as important as weight training regularly, or doing cardio regularly. We like to believe it is unimportant because, really, we don't see any 'visible' difference in the body. Interestingly, those who are inflexible and need it the most, avoid it the most. Improved flexibility improves other aspects of fitness, such as posture, demeanour and overall appearance.

It's a subtle thing but evident nevertheless.

Postural problems arise mostly because of the discrepancy between the flexibility and strength of opposing muscles. For example, if the chest muscles are tighter and stronger than the back muscles (opposing muscles), the shoulders tend to get rounded (because the chest muscles pull the shoulders forward) and drawn forward leading to 'the round-shoulder syndrome'. Something as simple as stretching the chest muscles (the pecs) and strengthening the back muscles (the lats, rhomboids, etc.) will solve the problem.

Anyone who has gone through a stretch routine will tell you how good it feels. Stretching does not lengthen the muscles. Muscles are attached to the bone at both ends making it impossible for that to happen, but it improves the elasticity of the muscles. This is especially important after a weight-training session when muscles are inclined to be tense.

Each muscle needs to be stretched differently and the stretch held for at least twenty to thirty seconds. Each muscle has a selection of specific stretches that can be done with varying degrees of difficulty, depending on your fitness levels.

Some studies show that stretching prevents injury. It certainly prevents pain and relieves Delayed Onset Muscle Soreness (DOMS).

When I train women and have them incorporate 'yoga' sequences into their routine to improve flexibility, I see some women are inherently more flexible. In fact, many Indian women are inherently more flexible. They manage to 'get into the pose', very easily.

But are they stronger, fitter, better? That is not always true. When they do start training with weights as well as doing yoga, they evidently become **stronger to stretch**, strange as that may sound. They stretch and get into poses with muscle control and confidence. They do not just 'flop' into the pose as they did earlier.

Flexibility is only *one* of the four pillars of fitness. Without the other three pillars—strength, cardiovascular and muscular endurance—it means nothing. A couple of yoga sessions a week seems to take care of flexibility for me. I would love to do more yoga, but just don't find the time with everything else.

There is a myth that weight training will make you inflexible.

Yes it will—if you do not stretch. You do not have to weight train for that to happen, just do not stretch enough and watch your body get inflexible. It amuses me greatly when people who do not train with weights, do not stretch and are extremely inflexible tell me that they do not want to train with weights because 'it will make them inflexible'.

Recap

- Muscles repair themselves and grow during the rest phase, not during the actual exercise.
- Without adequate sleep you are prone to weight gain, hypertension, fatigue, injury and other problems.
- There are several simple ways of ensuring good sleep by following 'sleep hygiene'.
- Adequate hydration is also an important part of staying healthy and being able to exercise.
- Adequate nutrition is clearly an important aspect of getting fit. An improperly nourished body cannot exercise.
- Losing fat and gaining muscle does not always happen simultaneously. As they both require very different

calorie intakes (to lose fat you need a calorie deficit and to gain muscle you need calorie surplus). They usually follow one after the other if the training protocols are done right.

- Stretching properly is part of the healing and recovery process. Incorporating yoga into ones routine helps in this respect. It is a huge myth that weight training causes muscles to become inflexible. It is 'not stretching adequately after weight training' that leads to tight muscles.

18

FOOD

Making Friends with Food

LISTENING TO YOUR BODY

'Eat well now because you won't get anything till lunch time'. I overheard a mother tell her ten-year-old who was insisting she was 'full' after eating just a little something for breakfast. The little one had been lazing around, so clearly, she wasn't too hungry. I don't think they had to fear a shortage of food in the near future and the little girl could easily choose to have a snack/fruit a little later if she was truly hungry. The mother, however, was concerned that she hadn't eaten 'enough'.

These are some of the confusing messages we are inundated with as children. We are told we *have* to eat, we are told *when* to eat and often *how much* to eat. Children are force fed at an early age. They are often given 'treats' to keep them quiet or entertained. As a result, we stop listening to our own bodies, disregarding signals of fullness and hunger because we believe we 'have to eat' way beyond what we really require. We are taught to ignore such valuable indicators from our body as feelings of fullness, discomfort, thirst as opposed to hunger, fatigue, sleepiness, anxiety and so on. **Over time, the body stops recognizing these signs for what they are and we struggle with an endless loop of overeating, lack of physical exercise, pills to sort out anything, from indigestion to anxiety, and are in a constant struggle with our weight.**

'Listening to our bodies' is a skill that seems to be lost to us as adults. Our physical and emotional selves are inherently very clever, telling us when we need to stop eating (we feel uncomfortably full), move more (we feel lethargic, full, bloated) or low on energy (we may be eating unhealthy, eating too little, or too much, exercising too much, sleeping too little, and so on). This skill needs to be nurtured from an early age.

It's not easy! Children can be fussy eaters, throw tantrums, and so on. It's a fine line between allowing a child to gauge her own hunger levels and stop eating when she needs to and allowing her to run wild, disregarding food on a whim. I don't suppose parenting was meant to be easy!

How often have we told our kids, 'Behave well and you will get a chocolate/ pizza/ burger?' Food has always been used as a form of emotional blackmail and persuading tactic. The result? **As adults we tend to seek comfort in food. We see food as our safety blanket and turn to it in times of stress, boredom, low mood and anxiety. We use it for more than just mitigating hunger.**

Take a buffet, for instance. How many of us can actually walk away from a buffet table feeling comfortable? How many of us wish later we had stopped just before than last piece of quiche or pudding? Our bodies *do* indicate to us when we have had enough, but we blithely eat 'just a little more', 'just to taste' something different or new. Children are encouraged to 'try everything' as we pile our plates astonishingly high and totter to and from the buffet table.

The problem occurs when this kind of behaviour becomes a habit. When we continue to eat 'just a little more' on a regular basis as our senses get blunted to our real needs. When we tell our children that they 'have to eat **now**', almost indicating that food will run out shortly.

SURVIVAL STRATEGIES

»   Eat mindfully. Be fully aware of what you are putting on your plate and in your mouth.

»   One of the ways of preventing weight gain is to stop eating when you are just 80 per cent full and leave the table. You can always snack later if absolutely necessary. You don't have to undo your jeans button in order to feel you have eaten well.

»   Serve yourself on a smaller plate. You will feel like you have a lot more food on it!

»   Don't eat in front of the TV or when distracted. You don't register what you are eating.

»   Make mealtimes pleasant and social with family/ friends when possible and keep it about having interesting conversation just as much as eating.

»   If you are done with your meal, get up from the table and walk away. Sitting around will tempt you to serve yourself more.

»   Stop telling yourself you are eating to please someone else. Whether it is your host, mother or mother-in-law or in-law, *they* cannot tell if you are full. Only *you* can ascertain that.

» You will also need to be educated and teach children about food groups, proteins, carbs, fats and micronutrients so you and they can make informed choices about food. That is more important than encouraging children to just 'eat well'.

» Be careful what you tell your kids. It's the programming at an early age that leads to difficulties with weight, food and body image later on.

FAD DIETS

If you are one to indulge in one of those 'fad diets' and have headaches, fatigue, missed periods, inability to sleep, and other such problematic symptoms please do not be led to believe that those are the signs of 'toxins being released' from your body. They are signs that you are not getting enough or the right kind of fuel for the proper functioning of your body. They are signs of your body protesting.

Do not allow yourself to be drawn into those murky waters of the cycle of yo-yo dieting, which leads to weight loss, transitions to overeating and is followed by the return of weight gain, which in most cases will be more than before. The cycle brings with it self-hate, depression, more dieting/binging.

Food is not the enemy. Make friends with it, understand it, understand your body's requirement for it and treat your body with the respect it deserves instead of alternately starving or stuffing it.

There is absolutely nothing wrong with liking, enjoying food and eating well.

A problem exists when you feel guilt and shame towards food. When that happens, you need to figure out *why* you feel that guilt and shame. Either you are eating unnecessarily or too much or indulging in the wrong thing (someone with high cholesterol levels will feel guilt when they eat, let's say, a rich creamy dessert).

Guilt and shame can also arise because we have been told that food is the enemy.

- That we should be on an eternal diet.
- That we should eat ourselves to a certain size.

Let your own body guide you. If it is responding well to the food you eat, if you have a healthy fat percentage, you exercise, meditate, feel energetic, look healthy, your skin feels plump and well moisturized, you enjoy your children and family and are productive through the day, then do not obsess about food.

EXERCISE DOES NOT GIVE YOU ENTITLEMENT OVER FOOD

Get over the sense of entitlement you feel towards food just because you exercise. It is true that exercising allows you to be able to eat what you like, but not indiscriminately. Exercising regularly will in fact give you a better sense of control over your food. Mastery over yourself and impulse control are some great spin-offs of exercise. You tend you plan your day around working out and plan meals accordingly. Seeing results will also encourage you to eat better.

Why would you want a special fad diet to 'lose weight'

when all you need to be healthy, and maintain a healthy weight, is there in right there in front of you...In your kitchen and in the local market. (If you have your own vegetable garden, even better).

» You *do not* need packaged concoctions (that cost an arm and a leg by the way) supplied to you three times a day.
» You do not need a powder or portion that pretends to be 'food' that you are supposed to mix with '1 per cent milk' to get *just* the right balance.
» You do not *need* to be told to eat five almonds and three gooseberries (just saying) to lose 'weight'.

Sometimes people ask some terribly silly questions, especially about diet and exercise.

• I drink lime juice and honey every morning. Will I lose weight?
• If I cut out my carbohydrates instead of exercising, is that better for weight loss?
• If I drink barley water will I lose weight?
• If I start working out and then stop, will I gain the weight?

If you do not want a sarcastic answer, do not ask an inane question.

I am often asked how to manage to get in four to five servings of vegetables a day. It seems like a difficult task for most people.

A serving is the equivalent of a cup of green leafy veggies, or half a cup of other regular veggies.

So that would mean that in order to get in four to five servings (for an average Indian woman), one would need to eat at least two cups of leafy veggies and one and a half to two cups of regular vegetables.

SEEMS LIKE A LOT?

Here's what you could do. At least at one meal a day, eat your vegetables first as a salad or soup. That way you ensure you get that done. Then your protein (chicken, lean meat, eggs, tofu, lentils) with some more stir-fried veggies. That should really be filling enough for one meal. Save the bread, cereal for another meal or if you are still hungry, eat one serving of the bread/cereal to accompany the protein.

The problem in most Indian meals is that we begin the meal with the bread/cereal and load up on easily as much as four to five servings of it in one meal, (Think two -and -a half cups of cooked rice; easily consumable in one sitting right? Especially if it is delicious biryani.) Then there is no space for vegetables and fruits.

If this is a constant scenario you *can* expect a widening waistline!

You should *learn* and *understand* food, food groups, food combinations, home-cooked wholesome food (not packaged junk, good-quality oils, whole grains, fresh veggies and fruit) and be able to work it out for yourself.

There will be the occasional lapses of judgement—all of us have them.

> *I accidentally consumed five biscuits when I wasn't paying attention. Those biscuits are wily fellows — they leap in like sugary ninjas.* — Charles Dickens

EMOTIONAL EATING

Food serves several purposes:

» To assuage hunger
» As a social connect between people when we enjoy a meal together as a family or with friends
» To nourish the body
» Repair and growth of the muscles and other tissues

It is, however, also used very often for another reason – for emotional comfort.

Think back to your childhood and you may recall that many a time, food was used as a bribe or a reward. This is ingrained so deep in our psyche that we continue to see food as a source of comfort. In our later years, when confronted with stress or pain, we tend to then turn to food for that same comfort.

The problem is, food cannot relieve the stress or pain. It, however, continues to be used as the one thing to turn to in various situations, including boredom, depression, anger, anxiety or even joy, happiness, satisfaction.

Using food in this way results in the weight gain that often only adds to the stress and pain (often physical and emotional). It is a viscious cycle. Emotional eating is an action, a habit. It does not define you. You can break it.

The next time you reach out to eat something, ask yourself, is this really physical hunger, or hunger of another kind that you need to deal with in a different way?

Recap

- Listening to your body is an art that we seem to forget as we grow older due to conditioning in childhood.
- There is absolutely nothing wrong with liking and enjoying food. When it takes over your life and you suffer guilt and shame or from eating disorders or obesity, that's when problems exist.
- Food is sometimes used to assuage stress, anxiety, boredom or depression. Unfortunately it cannot be of any help in these cases; in fact it only compounds the problem.
- We must, therefore, be very aware of the signals our body sends us from time to time telling us we are full/hungry/tired/anxious and so on and respond appropriately instead of using food as the universal solution.

19

THE THREE-STEP PROGRAMME

How to Do It?

STEP ONE: GET AN ASSESSMENT

Ascertaining the starting point is always important. It becomes easier to evaluate progress. Before you start an exercise programme, get an assessment done.

Medical Assessment

If you are over the age of forty get a clearance from your doctor. You would need to have some blood work done. Your blood sugar, cholesterol and thyroid function would need to be checked.

You will need your blood pressure tested and any specific complaints like back pain, knee swelling, chest pain and so on seen to.

A stress test on the treadmill or stationary cycle would be mandatory for anyone with a history of chest pain or discomfort, previous heart problems, family history of heart disease, history of sudden loss of consciousness (fainting), dizziness and unexplained breathlessness.

Fitness Assessment

Besides a routine baseline for height and weight, taking measurements with an inch tape at various points in the body like the hips, waist, chest and arms is necessary. It helps set the baseline for your current size. Thereafter, measuring the same points regularly when you are in the process of trying to lose weight will help you keep track of progress. Ideally, these measurements need to be taken by the same individual each time, preferably by yourself. That way, the chances of inter-observer variability are minimized.

The other areas where you will need to assess your fitness levels are stamina, strength and flexibility.

Observing how much longer you can walk, stand, run or even do housework can test endurance of the muscles or the ability to work for long periods of time.

Assessing Stamina: The First Pillar of Fitness

The One-Mile Walk Test is one of the many tests that assess your cardiovascular endurance or your stamina.

It is a simple test that evaluates the time taken to cover a distance of a mile or 1.6 km (usually on the treadmill or a flat walking path). Your heart rate is checked immediately after your walk and through a specific formula, your fitness level is assessed by evaluating what is called your **Vo2 Max.**

The Vo2 Max is the ability of your body to breathe and utilize oxygen for the working of the heart and muscles. Obviously, when you start exercising the body needs to be able to use oxygen efficiently and effectively, oxygen being the fuel of choice. The more efficient your body is in utilizing oxygen, the easier it is for it to exercise at a higher intensity. This is like a fuel-efficient car. Some cars are more efficient than others. They run better and longer on less fuel. Similarly, if you are fuel-efficient, your body (heart and muscles) is able to use oxygen as fuel efficiently, work harder and better without struggling (gasping for breath).

There are other tests like the *One-and-a-half Mile Run* or the *Swim Test* or *Step Test*, which could substitute the *One-Mile Walk Test*.

Once you have had your baseline Vo2 Max ascertained, you could re-evaluate it every couple of months to monitor progress. In addition to checking your weight and measurements, this re-evaluation helps you recognize and appreciate the different aspects of improvement of your body. Sometimes you may find that your weight or statistics have not changed too much over the last month. If those are the only two parameters you focus on, then you could be in for a disappointment, as weight and size do not decrease in a continuous linear fashion every month. There will be plateaus and there will be fluctuations.

If, on the other hand, you also assess your stamina, strength and flexibility and find that they have improved greatly over the same month, there is reason to take pride in what clearly is progress.

Assessing Strength: The Second Pillar of Fitness

Evaluating different muscles or muscle groups with the relevant exercises assesses their strength. Every fitness centre may have their own set of exercises.

The most common exercises done to assess strength of major muscle groups are:

Body Part	Exercise
Chest	Push-up or Chest Press
Back	Lat Pull Down
Shoulders	Shoulder Press
Legs and Glutes	Squats
Arms	Bicep Curls and Tricep Extensions

What is usually assessed is your *One Rep Max* or the maximum weight you can use to perform one single repetition of the exercise. Alternately, you could be asked to perform as many repetitions as you can, using a certain weight to maintain as a baseline for strength.

Assessing Flexibility: The Third Pillar of Fitness

Two or three exercises may be done to assess the flexibility of major muscles or muscle groups. Some common muscles tested are for the hamstrings, the shoulders and the spine and torso.

Hamstring flexibility can be tested by the *Sit-and-Reach Test*.

Shoulder flexibility may be tested by the *Shoulder Rotation Test*.

The spine and torso may be tested using the *Total Body Rotation Test*.

All these and many more fitness-assessment tests are sometimes performed to establish the baseline fitness levels of the individual before she starts training. If she has the right programme in place, all the pillars of fitness (stamina, strength, flexibility and endurance) will improve. One may not improve in all the aspects of fitness equally, uniformly or simultaneously. It is important, however, to see that they are all addressed so that there is a holistic development of the body.

Losing body fat alone to get as thin as possible should certainly not be the only objective of a fitness programme. Of what use is a thin/slim body if it is not strong and flexible as well? Similarly, of what use is a strong muscular body if it cannot climb stairs easily, run, walk, cycle or touch the toes, turn, twist and bend?

The ultimate objective of fitness should be a better body. More functional, more durable through wear and tear and more efficient. Better-looking is the bonus.

STEP TWO: START WORKING OUT

The next obvious step is to start working out. This is the most important part of the programme!

» **Cardio:** If you are an absolute beginner, walking even fifteen minutes a day will be a start. Increase gradually by five minutes every day until you reach a time limit of about thirty to forty-five minutes of cardio five days a week. Thereafter, you can try out other cardio classes if you want to add variety.

» **Strength:** Strength training and flexibility need to be started simultaneously with your cardio. Each pillar of fitness feeds off the other and makes each of them better.

Start with light weights and at least three to four days a week of weight training. That way, all the body parts may be addressed without being too pressed for time.

Set aside about half an hour per session for weight training. Gradually build your strength. Once you have learnt the exercises and can do them without injuring yourself, you may even cut it down to twice a week addressing all the body parts on each day. That way, you train the same body part at least twice a week.

»   **Flexibility:** Stretch every day at least for ten minutes. One or two long stretch or yoga sessions a week will greatly improve flexibility.

»   **Muscle endurance**: Go for a long walk or trek, play with the kids or play a game, run your dog, go for a leisurely swim over the weekend. This breaks the monotony of rigorous exercise through the week while keeping movement ongoing.

STEP THREE: CONTINUE WORKING OUT

This is the second most important part of the programme.
Re-evaluate regularly and revisit your diet.

This is probably also the hardest part of the programme. It seems like there is no end to it. There is not, that is the truth. You have to exercise for as long as your body allows it. However, continuing to work out should not necessarily impose boredom. You can change your routine. Sign up for a new class and so on to add variety. Besides, once you actually begin to enjoy working out (yes, that is possible) it is not something to complain about any more. You just do it.

Have a reassessment done every two to four months (earlier if you want to re-evaluate your routine and fitness). This keeps you motivated to keep going and make the necessary changes.

Fill a food journal and review it regularly. Consistently filling it for a couple of months will ensure that you understand clearly what is required of you. It also helps you understand food, make choices, observe your own eating habits and where you may be lapsing. The whole exercise of eating the right portions may seem complicated and daunting at first but it really is not. Once you get your head around serving sizes and food groups, it is very simple to eat holistic food to stay healthy and improve fitness.

FITNESS IS THUS A JOURNEY, NOT A DESTINATION

Everything changes with time, including your body. What you required at the age of eighteen is not the same as what you will need at fifty. The weights you use will change, the exercises you do should change, the amount of cardio you invest in will change too. This requires that you have someone to guide you, unless you have enough body awareness and body intelligence to continue on your own. Nothing is impossible. It does require you to be more in sync with your body, however.

As you continue to work out and work through your life's journey, exercising becomes an integral part of your life. So much that it is as simple as taking a shower; you fit it in any way.

'So can I stop once I lose weight?' Simran asked me when she came in for her first consultation.
'No,' I said.
'So, when can I stop?' she asked.
'Never,' I said.
She looked horrified.

'You mean I have to do this for the rest of my life?'

'Well, not exactly *this very* routine, but yes you have to exercise for the rest of your life in varying proportions and quantities.'

'Or else what?'

'You will face consequences like weight gain, lowered fitness levels, osteoporosis and so on.'

'Oh my god, maybe I shouldn't start!'

'That's like saying maybe I shouldn't eat now because I will be hungry again after a couple of hours.'

'Oh how depressing!'

'Does it occur to you that you may even enjoy it and not *want* to stop?'

She looked at me like I was crazy.

She started anyway. After two years of continuing to work out regularly, she actually loves it. She often wonders why she did not start earlier. Weight training is the favourite part of her workout.

Recap

- The Three-Step Programme:
  - ◆ Step One—Get an assessment (medical and fitness assessment).
  - ◆ Step two—Start working out.
  - ◆ Step three—Continue working out.
- There is unfortunately no way around it! Exercise is a 'lifestyle' not a short-term solution only to weight woes.

20

PSYCHOLOGICAL IMPLICATIONS OF WEIGHT LOSS

Losing Weight Is Not Just about Appearances

M uch research has been done to confirm the myriad benefits of losing weight. Predilection to various diseases including diabetes, heart disease, hypertension, even cancer is reduced with even moderate amounts of loss of weight. Losing weight, especially for the obese is beneficial. Adding regular exercise is even more beneficial.

The psychological benefits of weight loss have also been studied. The most common psychological problems faced by many overweight women are:

» Depression
» Lowered self-esteem
» Distorted, poor body image
» Eating disorders
» Low mood
» Lowered productivity

Clearly, body weight and size have strong associations with the psyche. Not only does the sheer discomfort of being overweight (associated back pain, immobility, knee pain, breathlessness, and so on) affect one's mood but just being overweight has psychological consequences. Unfortunately, our society does frown on obesity. As a result women who are obese or overweight tend to feel sidelined or excluded. Losing weight, therefore, has several psychological benefits.

Diet alone has been found to be unsuccessful in maintaining weight loss in the long term. It is next to impossible for women to follow stringent diets indefinitely. Besides, only dieting produces the most calamitous side effect of loss of muscle mass. As I have been reinforcing all through the book, improving and maintaining muscle is critical for one's well-being and fat loss.

Dieting is also detrimental to the mood. Low blood-sugar levels and hunger lead to irritability, depression, anxiety and an overall unpleasant personality. Being able to eat adequate (not excess) amounts of food and including exercise into one's day is far better than trying to starve oneself into a smaller size. Low-carbohydrate diets were found to affect memory when blood-sugar levels were low.

A preoccupation with food was another side effect of restrictive diets. Women then fantasize about food and spend several hours thinking about recipes, flavours, and so on. Binge eating and bulimia following these restrictive diets are common.

One study done in 2012, published in the journal *Metabolism,* found that repeated weight loss and gain did not, in fact, affect the woman's ability to lose weight again neither did it affect the benefits that weight loss had produced. The point is, why would we want women to go through cycles of dieting, weight loss and weight regain in the first place? Wouldn't it make more sense to find a straightforward way to lose weight and stay fit, even if slowly, and keep the weight off? Telling them it's alright to lose and gain weight repeatedly may just encourage them to do so.

Losing weight while dieting may be beneficial to her metabolic profile. How about her emotional and psychological profile when she regains her weight, generally more than the original weight? There is most definitely a cost to the negative psychological effects women experience with yo-yo dieting and 'weight cycling', as it is called.

A better way of dealing with obesity is establishing lifestyle habits of moderation and including regular exercise without the primary focus being solely on weight loss.

Women who 'diet' frequently (and I have known quite a number of them) and 'weight cycle' are very good at it. They have the capacity to stay on a diet for extended periods of time (but obviously not forever). So I do not believe there is a lack of 'will power' as is often asserted in these women. In fact, I think they have quite an abundance of will power. If this is somehow directed towards moderation in both food and exercise, then the results will be far better.

Instead of focusing on 'losing weight', improving fitness levels would be a more rewarding track to follow. Losing weight ensues any way. Regaining lost weight can be detrimental to one's psyche, setting one up for self-doubt, shame and guilt. All of this is a waste of valuable time and effort. Repeated cycles of similar emotions can be highly detrimental, as is expected.

Adding physical exercise, especially weight training,

is important for the long-term sustenance of weight loss, and also has several positive psychological benefits.

The very nature of exercise causes the release of endorphins in the brain, leading to an elevation in mood (unlike with dieting, which often causes the reverse). It is also found to relieve stress and anxiety. Working with one's body is extremely therapeutic as it gets you in touch with yourself and builds confidence.

Most of the women I have worked with claim to find the psychological benefits of exercise far more seductive than the actual loss of weight. There is no doubt that losing weight (which happens naturally when you exercise and eat right) is part of the allure. There will be times, however, when the scale moves little, if at all. Riding that plateau and continuing to exercise and implement positive lifestyle changes is aided by the mood-elevating effects of exercise itself.

Priya was a very large, angry woman when she joined TFL (Training For Life, which is a programme I started in 2000).

Large because she is five feet eleven inches tall and at that point, weighed a lot. Angry because of her troubled life and the difficulty she had coping with it.

When she joined she was also very skeptical about weight training.

Wouldn't she become 'larger'? Wouldn't she look 'manly'?

People had told her so. Maybe she should just do yoga?

She started training with weight nevertheless. She lost a ton of fat. Obviously, she is still very tall, but what a different person she is today. After two years of training regularly with weights (besides her cardio and stretches), she looks elegant, toned, young and terribly attractive.

But that's not all. Her life seems to have worked itself out. I suspect it has something to do with her own attitude. She is not angry at the world any more. She started running her own business. She is extremely confidant and a keen motivator for other women still sitting on the fence about weight training.

She says most women (and men) are still horrified when she tells them she lifts as much as she does very easily during her training. But she loves every moment and is such an inspiration to everyone else.

Women are, by nature more social than men. They enjoy group exercise, motivation, mentors and the social nature of any collective activity. That becomes part of their reason to continue to work out. Finding the right friends or group of friends to exercise with, registering with the right classes, becomes an important part of the process of change for them. A good support system goes a long way in maintaining regular exercise and diet. Healthy competition adds to the enthusiasm to keep at it.

I am not implying that *all* women need to join a group class or exercise together. Many are quite happy doing things on their own. Having a support system, at least in the initial stages, nonetheless helps to stay on track.

The increase in self-confidence in women who start to exercise, lose weight and transform themselves is quite remarkable. They begin to pay attention to themselves and take better care of their own bodies. They also seem to be able to extend their magnanimity to friends and family. Many believe losing weight, getting to be more mindful of themselves and being able to contribute something positive to their own well-being is the best mood elevator.

The spin-offs from this positivity and improved self-confidence are innumerable. They see an improved level of productivity, an increased interest in their own lives and that of those around them. The apathy that is often associated with obesity vanishes.

With this change in self comes several transformations from those around us. Some may feel unsettled by this improved persona. It may pose a threat to a relationship. Women often tell me stories about the negative attitudes of close family or friends concerning their weight loss and perceived 'difference' in their personality. Incidences of close family or friends sabotaging their efforts to stay on track with their diet and exercise are sometimes quite outrageous. This is an aspect of change that one needs to get used to and overlook. In most cases, others get used to the 'new you'. Those that do not should not matter. There will always be impediments along the way. Managing them well is part of successful change.

Recap

- Women who are over weight tend to face psychological problems like depression, lowered self-esteem, poor body-image etc. besides the physical and medical issues of obesity.
- Diet alone has not been found to be successful in long-

term weight loss. Although women on 'fad diets' often see results in the short term, these are not sustainable.

- It is the combination of diet and exercise (especially weight training) that will maintain fat loss.
- Dieting and the subsequent weight loss followed by weight gain is psychologically defeating. Find ways to keep the weight off instead. One of which is serious weight training.
- Eventually, it is the psychological benefits of regular exercise (the feel good factor) that keeps women coming back for more.
- Beware also that change in body and weight will create a reaction (not always positive) from those around us. Being prepared for it makes the transition and dealing with it easier.

21

STRIKING THE FINE BALANCE

The Art of Prioritizing

I never said working out regularly is an easy task. Many a time it has to be negotiated between the other occurences in life. If there is one quality, one personal characteristic that is most likely to produce results and is necessary for success, whatever the field, it would have to be the trait of **persistence.** Whatever else you may have – talent, good looks or a brilliant mind – persistence and the will to endure is what takes you far.

You also have to eventually find some forms of fitness you like to do if you want to stick with it. Not everyone likes everything. Personally, I am not particularly fond of the blazing sun, for instance, and find the outdoors difficult to survive for long periods of time. Therefore, outdoor activities or the midday sun may not be the best choice for me. Other people thrive in the sunshine. Some prefer dance-based workouts with music and exercises like aerobics, zumba, dancercise and salsa. Others like more athletic styles like step or martial-arts-based formats like kick-boxing. Still others prefer a solo walk or run to get in their cardio. There is a chapter in *Get Size Wise* called 'Determine your Fitness Personality'. That could give you a few tips in figuring out your preferred style of cardio.

You really do not have too much of a choice when it comes to weight training. Especially in the initial stages when you are learning the exercises. Aside from the fact that you can use barbells, dumb-bells, kettlebells or your own body weight to increase and improve muscle mass, you have to follow a certain series of exercises.

You need to train with weights a minimum of twice a week to maintain strength and muscle mass. To truly change your body shape and composition and build enough muscle, however, you will have to train most days of the week.

BASIC PRINCIPLES OF WEIGHT TRAINING

» Do not train the same muscle or groups of muscles again within twenty-four to forty-eight hours.
» Your routine will have to be planned in such a way that you train different groups of muscles every day and repeat the same group at least twice a week.

SETTING GOALS, MAKING RESOLUTIONS

Set goals and go after them. Goals or resolutions have to be realistic, however. One of the main reasons resolutions do not get followed through is because the very nature of the resolution is faulty. You resolve to lose weight in the new year. That is *not* a resolution. That is the *result*. Thus, in order to get that result you need to determine a *behavioural change*. What are *you* willing to do to achieve that result?

Your resolution should be something on these lines:

» Walk for forty minutes four times a week
» Train with weights twice a week
» Don't eat sweets during the week

These are behavioural changes that *you* can control. Your weight or the result is something you do not always have complete control over. Just deciding 'to lose weight' is not a resolution, that is wishful thinking.

STRIKING A BALANCE

Work, household duties, motherhood and social life always get in the way of exercise. Depending on priorities you are likely to add or delete your various responsibilities. Exercising regularly is a responsibility you owe to yourself. On some days, you may have to reorganize or even skip your workout routine altogether when there is an avalanche of work about to descend on you. This, hopefully, will happen only on rare occasions.

Striking a balance means trying to cope with the things you need to on a **priority basis**. Your sick child would obviously come before a party. Similarly, your workout should come before a casual social gathering.

Interestingly, I find the busiest women with careers, frantic social lives, travel and a home to deal with somehow manage to work out more often than women who are homebound with family obligations.

Perhaps it is their ability to:

» Clarify and organize time
» Say 'no' to unnecessary obligations

Perhaps it is their sense of self-preservation that prevents them from getting distracted and their ability to stay motivated about what is truly important. **After all, all of us have twenty-four hours a day. How we spend them is the key to what we achieve during the course of the day.** Always make a list of all the things you need to do.

At the other end of the spectrum, I do know women who allow fitness and exercise to completely take over their lives. I am not talking about those in competitive sport. For them, fitness is a career and a livelihood. I am referring to those women who use exercise like some use food or alcohol, as an escape mechanism or coping strategy. Some for whom exercising to extremes may be a symptom of something bigger. They exercise at the cost of everything else, including their health. Too much of a good thing (even exercise) can be a bad thing.

BODY DIMORPHIC DISORDER

Body Dimorphic Disorder (BDD) is a very real mental disorder. It is a psychological dysfunction where an individual exercises and diets to an extreme, believing her body to be imperfect. Most of us, I'm sure, would love to have a flatter stomach, straighter nose or slimmer thighs. But that does not and should not rule our lives. People with BDD **perceive flaws** in their bodies which completely consume them, causing severe emotional distress. They may resort to surgery, extreme exercise and diet, and so on to try and resolve the problem, which never gets rectified because it is their perception (of their body) that is flawed to begin with.

Their obsession with their appearance permeates every aspect of their life. They could endanger relationships, work, family and social connections with their fixation on appearance. These people need psychological help to change their cognition and behaviour to re-establish genuine priorities. The condition is often associated with depression, anxiety, or other mood disorders.

Striking a balance between real life; what we *think* we need to do and what we *have* to do can be quite an art. It is not always possible, neither is it perfect. Sometimes we feel we have let ourselves down.

I sometimes catch myself feeling disappointed in myself for not having trained on a given day. Then I have to step back and ask myself, was it laziness that prevented the apparent 'slip-up' or did a genuine disruption cause me to miss my work out (as there almost always is, quite frankly). I have learned to be kinder to myself. To appreciate what I manage to do and let go of the things I cannot.

Recap

- Working out regularly is not easy.
- Finding a form of cardio that you enjoy can keep you motivated.
- Strength training of course is non-negotiable.
- Setting goals is an art and should to be done with the help of a professional, if need be. Going after a goal and achieving it can keep you inspired to continue to exercise regularly.

- Striking the balance between working out regularly, your career, family, hobbies and fun is a fine balancing art.
- Body Dismorphic Disorder (BDD) is a mental disorder that needs to be addressed professionally.

22

TAKING RESPONSIBILITY, STAYING ACCOUNTABLE

Only YOU are Responsible for YOU

I have seen too many women fall prey to clever marketing and advertising that promise the perfect body. That is what sells. Women contribute to this walk down fantasy lane too. They choose to take the easy way out and do not question these miracle claims. They make excuses for themselves and play the victim, thereby renouncing control of their bodies and health.

I have serious reservations against women relinquishing control of their bodies to others or to society at large. I believe they need to sit up, take notice of themselves, and either be shocked or pleasantly surprised with what they see. Then, they should make the necessary changes to ensure that they progress, not regress.

This seems to be extremely difficult, almost impossible, for many. It is much easier to go to a dietician or a trainer and have her/him draw up meal plans or exercise routines for drastic and speedy results. If there is no 'weight loss', then conveniently the dietician/trainer is to blame. They are uninterested in the 'why', do not accept their own responsibility and are unwilling to question the methods used. They are not concerned with the long-term effects of rapid weight loss or starvation, as long as there are short-term results. They choose to believe what suits them rather than sieve the wheat from the chaff. **For instance, if someone says that drinking lemon and honey first thing in the morning helps 'burn fat', they would much rather believe and follow that than 'exercise first thing in the morning'!**

I believe women need to be more proactive about choices that concern their bodies. They need to be more discerning about long-term health, not just short-term cosmetic and health-related effects. They should protect themselves from falling prey to societal pressure to 'look' a certain way. It is not always possible to get to a 'certain size'. Much depends on genetics and environment, especially lifestyle, stress, work, and so on. Comparing oneself with another who is perceived to be 'beautiful' or 'slim' is a futile exercise.

Every woman is beautiful in her own way. She can also be the best possible version of herself physically and mentally by applying some basic principles of diet, exercise and healthy living. By challenging herself physically, intellectually and creatively, she can live a fuller and more fruitful life.

Women are more likely than men to allow emotional challenges to affect their eating, weight and health. Crisis in relationships or work can lead to abuse of food and ultimately the body. Binge eating, anorexia and bulimia are all psychological disorders with a foundation in lack of self-esteem and a troubled consciousness. Women are also more concerned about how society views their physical appearance. This translates into trying to 'look' a certain way. This self-defeating attitude can be highly corrosive to one's self-esteem.

There are most certainly several reasons (not just cosmetic) why being overweight is not discouraged, and why losing fat is advised. The reason to lose weight, therefore, should be focused more on health and not on mere looks. If you believe that just losing weight will make you feel better about yourself, you may be in for a surprise! You may feel ecstatic after the initial weight loss — the result of a sense of achievement, the admiration and applause from others and what you see in the mirror. After a while, when the compliments cease and the initial excitement wanes, you still need to find a good enough reason to continue with working out and implementing healthy eating habits. You need to find those resources from within yourself, and if you are lucky, from encouraging friends. Herein lies the difference between short-term weight loss and long-term achievements. **Everyone struggles to lose weight and get on track. Staying on track and keeping the weight off is more difficult.**

Being fit is not just about being a certain size, but achieving an improved level of performance of the body and a superior-quality life. It is the understanding of this journey that keeps you experimenting, progressing and enjoying the process enough to persist with it for as long as you possibly can. It becomes a way of life, so much a part of your day that it is no more an ordeal to exercise. It is your way of saluting your body, of respecting it, and rewarding it for being there for you!

Women need to love their bodies more. Be thrilled,

amazed and appreciative of it. They need to stop abusing it with food or lack of exercise. They need to understand that they are already beautiful but can become even better versions of themselves if they only try.

'Can you really learn to *love* to exercise?'

This is an incredulous question I often get. Well, if you do not learn to *love* it, at least learn to *like* it.

Let's face it—you really don't have a choice. So whether you learn to love it or not, you simply have to **just do** it. If you do it long enough, it grows on you. You get better at it. Even excel. You miss it when you do not work out. You enjoy pushing your limits. You appreciate yourself more. You organize your day around your workout, even managing to squeeze it into your lunch hour if necessary. You make friends accordingly. You plan activities around it. If you have a favourite television show you just cannot miss, wouldn't you work everything around it? Well...Think of this as your *absolutely* favourite television serial with you as the star.

Make friends with people who like fitness and lead a healthier lifestyle. It has been found that your friends, family and society greatly influence the choices you make. Associate with people who make the healthier choice consistently. This ensures positive influences on you and makes it easier for you to stay motivated. On the other hand, being surrounded by unhealthy options all the time, family and friends who binge and are careless about their own health makes it that much more difficult to stay on track. Especially in the initial stages, where inspiration is an issue, stick around people who motivate you positively.

There comes this point in your life when you want to do away with all the drama. With unnecessary connections and relationships that cause more anguish than joy. Things that are truly a waste of precious time. You want to spend more time doing meaningful things, for yourself and a few deserving others, contributing in the best possible way you can without inconsequential interruptions. You want to spend more time with yourself, with people who make you laugh, with people who really matter, with people who value you for what you are and support you in the best possible way.

Do not underestimate the psychology of getting into and staying with a fitness routine. It is not always as simple as, 'just do it'. Very often you have to trick your body. Sometimes it is just not inspiring to get up in the morning to go for that bike ride or run. Sometimes you just don't feel like lifting those weights.

AT SUCH TIMES THE KEY IS TO HAVE A BACKUP PLAN

» Coordinate with a friend to go for an early morning walk so you feel obliged to go when she messages you even if you would rather lie in.
» Sign up for a class. Make some friends amongst the students so there will be some reminders and pressure for you to go even on days you are not up to it.
» Hire a personal trainer who will wake you up cheerfully early in the morning to take you through your routine.

You may need some strategies to keep yourself enthused and committed. As time goes by, however, it becomes something you look forward to. The most important thing is to first believe that you can. If none of the above help, well, you really have to **just do it**!

Irresponsible behaviour gets mimicked over time. Exercising is initially a process of self-improvement, to get healthier, lose weight and feel better. Eventually, however, it has several ramifications within your family and friends. Mothers set examples for their daughters. She cannot, for example, expect her daughter to lose weight when she does not set a good precedent. A mother who believes in healthy living, tends to also cook healthy and be conscious of what she puts on the table for the family.

Outside interference is something to watch out for. Other people, even complete strangers, may appear to have a keen interest in your weight, exercise and food. They may for instance say, 'But you don't need to lose any more weight', when they see an apparently 'slim' person exercise.

It is not just about weight loss. Only someone who works out understands the sense of well-being, accomplishment, control, satisfaction and joy it brings. Weight is only a small part of the equation. After a point, weight stops being the most important aspect of working out.

A client came to me one day to tell me she would not be able to attend her fitness sessions for a week on account of the Diwali celebrations. She had to help make the sweets at home, help distribute them, then there were the never-ending guests and social gatherings to attend.

'Was that ok?' she asked me.

'No,' I said.

She looked very troubled.

'But I have to be at home, I have to do all these things.'

'That's fine,' I said. 'Go ahead.'

'But you said it was not ok.'

She looked confused.

'No it's not, but you say it's what you **have to do**, so go ahead.'

'If you say it's ok, then I will feel happier,' she replied.

There is a situation in medical practice where, when a patient has not recovered fully but wants to be discharged for whatever reason, she or her family will sign an 'Against Medical Advise' clause. They can most certainly be discharged, but not according to medical advice or protocol. When the patient does this, she and her family essentially have to take responsibility for their actions and consequences.

It's the same with exercise. If you choose not to exercise for whatever reason **(yes it is a choice)**, then you **take responsibility and stay accountable to yourself**.

Someone else condoning it or not really doesn't make a difference.

Recap

- It is important to take responsibility for your own body and health.
- This would mean not subjecting it to unnecessary stress and trauma of fad diets and miracle cures looking for short-term solutions.
- Every woman is beautiful in her own way.

- She should focus on being the best possible version of herself and not someone else and certainly not the dictates of society.
- Being slim/thin alone is not sufficient. It is more important to be healthy, get fitter.
- To sustain regular exercise, choose your influences well. Friends who lead a healthier lifestyle tend to be more supportive of your journey.
- Always have a backup plan for your exercise.
- Over a period of time you will actually learn to enjoy it. This happens particularly when you begin to excel at it.
- You should stay accountable to yourself. Expecting others to condone or praise you all the time is a self-defeating attitude.

23

FAQs IN WEIGHT TRAINING FOR WOMEN

All Your Weight-Training Questions Answered

The basic principles of weight training have already been elaborated on in my first book, *Get Size Wise*. Here I will go through some of the common questions women always ask me about training or wanting to train with weights.

» **Will I get 'masculine' and 'muscular' if I train with weights?**
Masculine, no.

Masculinity (with male features, voice, hair growth, and so on) is the result of the hormone testosterone, which men have infinitely more of circulating in their body. Just training with weights will not increase testosterone or masculinity.

Muscular, yes. Your muscles will increase in size and strength when you train with heavy weights. In order to see muscle definition, however, the layer of fat over the muscle should be limited if there at all. Most women who train with weights as recreation (not as a body-building sport) usually do not get to the point of looking ripped and muscular simply because that takes a lot more effort, training and a special diet to lose body-fat percentage. They tend to look more toned and shapely if they train right.

» **At what age should I start training with weights?**
Ideally own-body-weight exercises should be started from an early age, as young as eight or ten years. Serious training can be started in early adolescence using moderate weights and under supervision. It is a myth that growth gets restricted if teenagers participate in weight training.

» **Do I need to be fit before I start weight training?**
Not necessarily. A very unfit person can start weight training, initially using very light weights. Needless to say they have to be supervised diligently. They should simultaneously include cardio into their routine to burn more calories. Walking, cycling, low-impact floor-aerobic classes are all acceptable.

» **What about the pain you experience after weight training? How do I deal with that? It is discouraging.**
The pain or soreness you experience about twenty-four hours following a weight-training session is called Delayed Onset Muscle Soreness (DOMS). It is caused by the small micro tears in the muscle fibres during the training session. The healing of these tears is what causes DOMS. These healed fibres are stronger than the untrained muscle. One gets used to DOMS.

Honestly!

A seasoned weight trainer is not troubled by DOMS. In fact they rather appreciate that they actually recognize the existence of certain muscles in their body that they never even knew existed.

A warm-up and cool down during sessions and a stretching and a warm bath following sessions help with DOMS. You don't need to be alarmed or discouraged by it.

» **How many sets and reps should I do per exercise?**
Anywhere between eight to twelve repetitions is advised to build strength and size of muscle. You need to do at least three sets per exercise. With a heavier weight you will be able to complete only about eight repetitions.

» **Which is better—free weights like dumb-bells and barbells or machines?**
Both have their unique advantages and disadvantages. Free weights allow for more freedom of movement and calls into play some amount of core strength and balance. But chances of injury are more with free weights.

Machines have a restricted movement pattern. Chances of injury are less with the machines. Using both is advisable to gain the benefits of their advantages.

» **What about own-body-weight exercises? Are they better than using dumb-bells/barbells/machines etc?**
They are different and have their own advantages. When you do own-body-weight exercises like push-ups, pull-ups and squats you learn how to handle your own weight. Sometimes, however, you will be unable to handle your own body weight, as it may be too much for your muscles. Increasing strength using dumb-bells, barbells and machines initially by building strength gradually will make own-body-weight exercises easier.

I recommend doing both.

» **How do you differentiate between DOMS and pain from injury?**

This is a very pertinent question. DOMS always arises in the muscles not in the joints and usually about twenty-four hours after a workout. Pain from injury usually appears immediately after a workout and may even arise from the joint.

Ultimately, you have to train with weights long enough to understand and be able to clearly differentiate any untoward pain. DOMS usually disappears within about forty-eight hours. Any pain that persists, is very uncomfortable or causes severe restriction of movement has to be addressed by a professional.

» **How can I prevent injury while training with weights?**

Keen body awareness and body intelligence is necessary to prevent injury. Unfortunately, not everyone starts training with that level of body intelligence. This is why a good personal instructor is a great advantage. She will be able to recognize mistakes you make or are likely to make even before you do. This is why being an attentive learner is also crucial to preventing injury.

With time, however, one gets to understand one's body better. You learn to recognize subtle signs and refrain from pushing harder than necessary. You appreciate the signals your body sends you and you stop yourself going beyond your capabilities.

» **How often should I train with weights?**

For a busy woman trying to build in strength and muscle mass, a minimum requirement of weight training would be twice a week addressing all the body parts. This means you train each body part twice a week. Every session will need to be about sixty minutes long.

» **How much weight should I lift?**

No one else can determine how much weight you lift! Only *you* can determine that. You will also need to lift a different amount of weight for different muscles. You start with a weight with which you can complete ten to twelve repetitions per set of each exercise. You should not be able to do more than ten to twelve repetitions. This weight will differ for each exercise. You will, for instance, be able to lift a heavier weight while doing shoulder presses compared to a bicep curl simply because the shoulder press uses a larger muscle (the deltoid) capable of handling more weight than the bicep muscle which is much smaller.

You will gain rapidly in strength in the initial stages. You will find that the weight you choose to perform ten to twelve repetitions increases rapidly initially, till you reach a kind of plateau. Thereafter, increase in strength is more gradual if you keep training. You will reach a point where you know you don't want to, or need to, build more muscle. You should then maintain that weight you train with.

» **How and when do I increase the weight I use?**

When the weight you are using becomes too light for you and you are able to easily complete twelve or more repetitions it may be time to increase the weight for that particular exercise. On an average, women should train using weights which allow them to do not more than ten to twelve repetitions for each set of the exercise.

This is true especially of those starting out with weight training. Heavier weights with lower reps can be started after one is familiar with the exercise form.

» **What happens if I stop training with weights?**

When you stop training you stop gaining muscle and if you do not use those muscles you have built, they will atrophy (or become smaller). They are never replaced by fat. Fat and muscle are two different types of tissue, like chalk and cheese, and one cannot become the other. You may, however, gain fat as a separate eventuality if you continue to consume the same number of calories you did while you were training. As the energy balance will obviously be skewed in favour of increased consumption as opposed to expenditure, the result will be fat accumulation. The combination of loss of muscle (due to disuse) and gain of fat (due to overconsumption and decreased energy expenditure) will lead to a flabby-looking body.

Once you build enough strength and muscle tone, you don't need to spend hours training if you do not wish to or cannot for logistical reasons. Even sixty minutes twice a week is sufficient to sustain strength and muscle mass.

» **Can I lose fat in one particular area by training it over and over again?**

In other words what you are asking is, 'Is spot reduction possible'?

No. It has been found that spot reduction does not exist. When you train one area, for instance, do endless bicep curls, the biceps become bigger but fat over the biceps alone does not disappear.

» **Can I get a flat stomach by doing ab exercises alone?**
The question is similar to the one above. Does spot reduction work? No, it does not. Doing hundreds of ab exercises without doing anything else will not get you a flat stomach. In addition, if you do some cardio, train the other parts of your body with weights to increase muscle and watch your diet, you will eventually get that flat stomach.

» **If I do side bends and ab crunches with weights will my stomach get flatter and waist get smaller faster?**
You don't need to use weights to do your ab exercises. Ab muscles that lie on the abdominal wall are very slim and flat. The objective is to get a flat stomach and strengthen these muscles and not build their size. You do not want a thick waist with large muscles. Do not do weighted ab exercises. Your own-body-weight exercises, (sit-ups, crunches, reverse crunches and the bicycle) are excellent exercises for the abs done without weights.

» **What happens if I do not train with weights at all?**
Women who do not train with weights tend to lose about half a kilo of muscle per year, for every year after the age of thirty. This, of course differs between women, the muscle loss being less in those who tend to be active physically, lifting, pushing, doing house work, carrying heavy bags, and so on, on a regular basis. For those majority who do not do much physical work to speak of, the muscle loss will be much more rapid and obvious. The result is a flabby body (even if slim) with a higher fat percentage and low lean-body mass.

Muscles, as I have described, are very important, not only for the proper functioning of the body but also for aesthetic appeal. A firm, toned body appears more youthful.

» **How soon after surgery can I train with weights?**

It takes about six weeks for surgical wounds to heal provided there is no post-operative infection, anaemia or general malaise. Following abdominal surgery, as after a hysterectomy or caesarean, one needs to first stabilize and control the abdominal muscles with breathing exercises. This can be started within a week to ten days of surgery when the soreness has decreased.

Start with simple core strengthening exercises like plank, side plank, and T-stand. These strengthen the core muscles without putting undue stress on the surgical wound. After six weeks, one can certainly begin weight training again, starting with lighter weights to build up to original strength. When one resumes weight training for the rest of the body, care should be taken to engage the core and keep it stable. Proper breathing and technique is paramount.

» **How long should my weight-training routine last?**

That depends on how much time you have and how many days you can dedicate to weight training. All the muscles of the body can be worked in an hour. Obviously, this will be a high-intensity workout. In order to complete the routine in one hour, there is very little rest between sets and no time to lose. If you work the whole body in a single day, performing at least one to two exercises per body part, then the routine can be repeated twice a week.

On the other hand, if you have only half an hour a day but can train four or five days a week, then different body parts can be addressed on different days, doing more exercises per body part.

Training routines can be tailored to your requirements, goals and time available. A clever trainer will be able to manipulate the routine in such a way that it benefits you best.

» **How many exercises should I do per body part?**

Once again this depends on your goals. For more muscle definition, at least four to five exercises per body part, and five to six sets per exercise will be required. Each set should have only six to eight repetitions.

For a general weight-training routine for health and fitness, two exercises per body part should suffice. You should, however, lift heavy enough weights. Do ten to twelve repetitions for each set.

» **What about boot camp, crossfit and other such exercises?**

Boot camp and Crossfit evolved as forms of strength training, which are done in a particular format (usually very intense, no rest, highly challenging exercises). Such workouts not only save time but also act as cardio. **These are not for everyone, however.**

The important thing is to first be highly proficient in all the basic weight-training exercises, know how to perform them flawlessly before attempting these advanced protocols. Chances of injury are higher in such forms of fitness due to the higher intensity, lack of rest, and so on. One must therefore have a high degree of body awareness and a strong foundation of strength if one wants to prevent injury.

These are great ways of staying fit. They may be repeated only twice or thrice a week to prevent overuse injury. Adding stretching, yoga, moderate-paced walking for a better-rounded routine will help balance your fitness.

» **When do I stop weight training?**

You do not!

One can continue to train right up to a ripe old age as long as one is training carefully. When the muscles are challenged and stimulated they remain toned, firm and functional. Frailty of old age which in turn leads to loss of balance, falls, invalidity, and so on are the result of poor muscle function. The only way to prevent this is to work the muscles against resistance and keep them challenged.

» **Can I do weight training exercises at home?**

Sure you can.

Ensure, however, that you first learn all the exercises and are able to do them flawlessly. If you learn all the basic exercises, all you need are a couple of dumb-bells, a barbell with plates and a mirror at home so you can work at your convenient time.

You must remember, however, that training alone regularly calls for a high degree of motivation. If you are not likely to stay self-motivated, it may be better to get yourself to a gym where there are other people and a trainer to encourage you.

> Often, when I give talks to groups of women about the importance of starting a weight-training programme, the inevitable conversation ensues:
>
> 'When I stop weight training will I become "flabby"?'
>
> 'Are you toned and in great shape now?'
>
> 'No'. 'So what have you got to lose? You start training, get firmer and more toned. If you stop, you are back to what you are now.'

» **Why do most women shy away from weight training?**
Most women think weight training is only for men. They also falsely believe that doing cardio and yoga is sufficient. If you want a toned, better-looking body and if you want to build strength and muscle, you have to train with weights. Building strength and muscle is extremely beneficial.

» **Why are women so afraid of weight training?**
Perhaps they do not understand what it is really all about. When you do not understand something you are afraid of it. They visualize bodybuilders with huge muscles and imagine they will get that way if they so much as pick up a barbell. Truth is, it is very difficult to build large muscles. It takes hours of training (and sometimes steroids and other unnecessary supplements) to be a competitive bodybuilder. Recreational weight training is very different. We use lighter weights and train moderately to build muscle, and at the same time, keep injuries at bay.

» **If I start training with weights and stop for a while, what do I do?**
Start again!

» **Do I always need a personal trainer?**

Initially, I would advise a trainer to teach you the basics. Once you learn the basics of weight training, other exercises are very simple to learn. You can then train on your own or in a group setting. You have to be highly self-motivated to train on your own. Some women just aren't. You will need to see a fitness consultant from time to time to change your routine, tweak it and improve on it.

» **Do I need to keep changing my weight-training routine?**

You do not. Just increasing the weight used in basic weight-training exercises is sufficient to see improvement. Exercises are changed and routines altered mainly to prevent boredom and add challenge.

» **Is there an age limit to training with weights?**

It has been found that starting a weight-training programme even at the age of eighty is beneficial. You can start at any age, provided it is under expert guidance. One has to keep in mind the frailty of the body, the possibility of osteoporosis, arthritis, and other similar maladies when training older women. Older women who continue to train with weights are much stronger, more shapely and their body more toned and youthful.

» **If I do enough cardio (like training for and running a marathon, for instance), should I also train with weights?**

That's like asking, if I eat enough rice, should I also eat protein. Of course you should. Stamina (with cardio) and strength are two different pillars of fitness and both need to be addressed. How much of each, how often, how hard, and so on needs to be individualized by a qualified professional in the field.

»   **What is the difference between weight-training and resistance training?**

They are one and the same thing. To improve strength and muscle mass, you have to challenge the muscles. How you challenge them can vary. **You can use any form of resistance to challenge your muscles.** It may be in the form of free weights, machines, own-body-weight exercises, the TRX (which uses your own body weight), various forms of boot camp (which is only a specific format for doing the exercises), and other such means. Resistance training only means you use external resistance.

24

AFTERWORD

Wabi Sabi

'Wabi Sabi' is a Japanese ideology. The very sound of the word enchanted me. Researching it, I discovered the implied philosophy to be rather appealing. It states three simple realities:

» Nothing is perfect.
» Nothing is permanent.
» Nothing is finished.

But you make peace with it.

I think this is terribly relevant to health, weight, size, fitness, beauty and wellness. If you look at the philosophy casually, it seems to imply that you accept the deterioration of your body or consider obesity, ill health and disease a natural part of ageing and make peace with it. You could say, for instance:

» Since nothing is perfect, why bother trying to make it so?
» Since nothing is finished, why bother starting?
» And since nothing is permanent, what is the point of

attempting to stay fit or improve health?

To me, however, it embodies something else altogether. **It signifies the very essence of taking care of oneself for the right reasons and by using the right methods.**

I believe **nothing is perfect.** Life situations are never perfect. You make the best of it.

Sometimes you may not have the time to exercise, you may be travelling or you may have sick kids to contend with. You may work long hours, be stressed and living under the pressure of deadlines. You do not always **have** the time. You **make** the time. That is just what you do when something is important enough in your life. It is what you do when something is top priority.

Even a twenty-minute workout at home is better than nothing at all if you cannot get to the gym. A quick run on the treadmill or a swim in the pool in your hotel while you are travelling is better than sulking about your endless travel and how it impedes your fitness.

You may be obliged to attend lunches and dinners. This certainly does affect your diet resolutions, but instead of sampling everything on the menu and living with the guilt, strategize how to eat out sensibly. Weigh your food options and make reasonable choices at every meal. Compensate for an indulgence by having a few light meals and making sure you work out.

These are coping mechanisms that clever women use to stay on track.

Of course life throws you a curve, all the time!
What takes us through and out on the other side with some semblance of sanity is our self-confidence.

Although a support system around us helps to ease the process, it is the belief in ourselves that is the game-changer.

THE MYTH OF PERFECTION

We are also confronted with another kind of perfection that often gets in the way of regular women exercising for themselves and to improve their health, mood and quality of life.

We have been programmed into believing in perfection. More importantly, the kind of physical perfection portrayed by the media and largely by the western world. Not everyone can look like the model on the cover of a magazine, not even the model on the cover of the magazine, and neither should we try.

Trying to look like somebody else is a wasteful exercise. Trying to adhere to the dictates of society to be a certain size or appear a certain way will not necessarily get you a healthier body. It is more likely to cause you a lot of angst and frustration.

Spend your energy carefully and wisely. You only have a limited amount of it per day. If you spend it:

» Stressing out about what has not been achieved, or how you look or do not look
» Worrying unnecessarily about the opinions of others,
» Re-living past melodrama

You will not have the energy to enjoy the moment and make it more meaningful. You will not have the energy to actually do things to improve your health and wellness.

The best way to lose fat is to *not* obsess about it.

Instead of watching your weight, counting calories, exercising maniacally, talking endlessly about it and worrying about not losing weight all the time, **spend time establishing healthy life habits:**

» Eat mindfully after understanding food, food groups, and supplements.
» Exercise sensibly (longer duration is not necessarily better).
» Stay active through the day.
» Stay interested and excited in what you do on a day-to-day basis, whether it is housework or a career in nano technology.
» Take time off to relax, play with the kids/dogs, meet a friend, meditate and contemplate.

The fat loss will happen anyway if you do things right.

Nothing is permanent. Life changes. We change. We age. That is the normal physiological process. Yet, youth is revered. Even when we know it is never permanent, we strive to hang on to it with our teeth and the tips of our fingernails. The tremendous surge in clientele for botox, laser, face lifts, tummy tucks and so on are testimony to our infinite need to stay young and beautiful.

The chapter 'The Anti-Ageing Pill' is not advocating that one has to look young all your life. The fact is, increasing and improving muscle mass and strength does make for a younger, healthier body, and a body that can withstand the ageing process better. A body that can deal with the vulnerabilities of ageing and better still, prevent them altogether. Ageing gracefully is an art. Keeping your body strong while growing intellectually and spiritually is not the same as trying to hold on desperately to one's youth. Work with the flow rather than against it. Rather, invest in **building strength, maintaining stamina and improving flexibility.**

Understanding that nothing is permanent is what should keep us moving forward. Even good health, a great body, astounding intellect or superior athletic capability is not permanent unless you continue to work at it. Honing your skills, practising, staying with the programme, persisting and staying on top of things to maintain and improve oneself is imperative to be successful.

Even elite sportspersons know that their athletic prowess declines with age. Our bodies change in a myriad ways as we age and we need to look at ways of working towards bettering ourselves. We may not be able to run a marathon in our latter years (although some do), but we will be able to continue exercising, to strengthen our bodies and keep ourselves free from disease. We do not have to succumb to obesity or ill health resulting from poor lifestyle habits.

In my work as an obstetrician and gynaecologist, I have spoken to thousands of women over the years from different social strata, ages, shapes and sizes, and who are in different stages of their lives and whose lives I have followed for a long time, giving me insight into their events and growth process.

» Teenagers — some rebellious, troubled; others eager to see what life has in store for them.
» Young women about to be married, excited sometimes scared.
» Pregnant women with their own assortment of

problems, some completely relaxed, taking it as it comes, others — Google scholars — who come in with a huge file of Internet research and queries.

» Mothers with sick kids or with their own physical problems.
» Older women facing empty-nest syndrome, depressed, anxious.
» Women, who have grown into their own, coming to terms with life and their circumstances.

There is a common thread among those women who mostly seem to come out on top, or at least are in some way in control of their own lives and/or decisions they make. It is the level of genuine self-confidence and a true desire to improve, introspect and move forward. At the same time, it is the ability to also roll with the tide that makes women better at handling 'life'. Things happen, you compromise, you change, you move on!

I have seen this in rural women as often as in someone from the higher socio-economic urban background, irrespective of how they look or their educational achievements. With age comes wisdom (hopefully) to differentiate between impractical claims and an authentic method of staying fit and healthy.

» When you come to value your body for what it can do rather than simply what it looks like.
» When you start to appreciate how unique your body is.
» When you start to actually *listen* to it, give it what it *needs* not just what you *want*.
» When you stop punishing it for not looking the way you think it is supposed to.
» When you use exercise as a way to celebrate and enjoy

your body's capabilities.

» When you are thrilled in the aftermath of a long, strenuous weight-training session or feel the joy of quivering legs after a run.

If and when you go through these emotions, fitness for you will have become a way of life and not just a means to an end and this in itself is a gift.

At some point, at some level we tend to believe we are victims of circumstances. Be it upbringing, programming, religion, politics, lifestyle, education, monetary status, marriage, children, profession, or even where we live. Yet at some point, at some level we need to accept that we *can* be what we *choose* to be. It is, however, not always the easy choice.

> *I am not what happened to me,*
> *I am what I choose to be.* – Carl Gustav Jung

Accepting the imperfect, impermanent and unfinished nature of everything and yet staying motivated to continue to improve one's body, mind and life, this attitude that allows a semblance of peace within us is one of coming to terms with a situation. This is because **nothing is finished**. The human body is a work in progress. We usually start exercising with simple goals:

» Lose 10 kg
» Get into that dress
» Run a marathon
» Trek to the Himalayas

Once we achieve those goals we must continue to include fitness in our day, hone our skills, change our routine to make us better and try new forms of exercise. We are in a hurry to perfect and finish the process. We forget that the process itself is part of the journey and is more relevant than the end point. The journey is the 'now', the destination is the 'future'. We are in a hurry to lose weight, to reach the destination faster. We find ways to do it quickly, shabbily and with no regard for the true physiology or functioning of the human body. **We fail to understand that as humans, we can never be a finished product, perfect or permanent**. If we lead mindful lives, our bodies will be ever-changing, evolving and progressing. Thus **fitness is a journey, not a destination**.

I remember, as children when we drove to places on holiday, every kilometre or so one of my sisters or I would ask the interminable question, 'When do we get there?' All the while my mother tried to distract us with the animals, the fauna and flora by the roadside, regaling us with the beauty of the place, trying to tell us that the journey was as much a part of the holiday as was getting to the holiday spot. I am often reminded of that expression of childhood exasperation and impatience when clients are in a rush for me to give them a deadline. Or when they are in a hurry to see results.

One of the nicest mails I received from a reader of my first book was:

Dear Doctor,
I was always looking for ways to lose weight. Reading your book made me understand that losing weight alone should not be the priority. Getting fit should. That it's a journey not a destination. Thank you for the inspiration.

In our quest for weight loss and looking better we tend to lose perspective. Understanding the bigger picture that losing weight should not be the one and only priority is what keeps people from falling off the wagon. **If people spent half as much time focusing on their health and fitness as much as they do in attending to their physique, they will be much better off and more successful at it.**

I tell women, 'You have to start working out with your body by appreciating it first.'

Appreciating your body does not mean you 'let it be' in the shape or size that you have allowed it to degenerate to. It does not mean you allow it to get overweight or unfit. It means that you respect it and treat it with kindness. It means you find the right exercises and adequate nutrition to supply it with in order to keep it well nourished, in good health and improve its condition. Thus, balance and moderation are the keys to longer-lasting success.

Ridiculous, extreme diets and exercise schedules may produce dramatic short-term results. How long can these results be sustained? How long can the body be put through rigorous forms of near torture and not rebel?

Feeling defeated by a few setbacks and giving up at the first signs of difficulty is a sure way to take two steps forward and three steps back. This could well be a pattern for some. Pick yourself up and move on! The difference between those who manage to stay on track despite the hurdles and detours in their way is purely their belief in themselves that they *can*!

EPILOGUE

I am constantly amazed at the number of women who *do not* train with weights or perform own-body-weight exercises to improve strength and muscle mass. There is so much evidence regarding the benefits of weight training that it seems like such an obvious decision to make; **to start weight training**.

Life is more than just a number on the scale.

The most common reason women come to consult with me as fitness and lifestyle consultant is — 'I want to lose weight'.

I rarely hear, 'I want to get fit'.

You really *are* more than just a number on the scale. True, these numbers are a reference point (from a health perspective), but that is all they are. You do not walk around with your weight written on your forehead or hung like a placard around your neck. Unless you are an athlete or sportsperson, where weight is an integral part of the screening and qualifying process, no one really judges you by your weight on the scale. What you are judged by, unfortunately, is your size and the way you look.

The tragedy is that overweight people are often categorized as lazy or slow. We need to stop body shaming. Making others feel bad about their own bodies is not the most productive way to help them make changes. Mothers bring their daughters to me claiming the child is fat and needs to lose weight. The young girl, often with downcast eyes has already felt the pain of rejection and body shaming as a result of her size. This is no way to enter womanhood. Instead, joining her and encouraging her in her journey through fitness will help both mother and daughter.

Feeling bad about oneself is the worst way to start a healing relationship with the body. Although I agree it can be the motivating factor that brings one forward to start an exercise and healthy-eating programme to begin with, a continued negative attitude towards your body will not take you far.

You do need to be driven and disciplined if you want to see real change in your size. Consistency and persistence are the only qualities that pay. While being consistent with an exercise routine and eating clean for the most part is important, it is equally important not to let life go by.

I find women who start exercising also begin enjoying life more. Perhaps it is the elevation in mood that regular exercise brings. Or perhaps, it is the increased levels of confidence in oneself. The emotions spill over into other aspects of life. Women become more adventurous, bold, excited and open to try new things. All this happens if they are in a nurturing environment during the process of their change.

That is the ideal scenario. However, it does not always play out that way. I see several gymnasiums where women are made to feel worse. They are subtly ridiculed, even by the trainers. They are made to feel like failures if they do not manage to make the scale move. In their homes, they are mocked by their husbands. Siblings or acquaintances

(I can hardly call them friends) tease or sneakily deride other women.

Women are not entirely blameless either. Many walk around like unanswered questions, seeking opinions, wanting approval. They set out to change their bodies for the sake of a significant other. 'My boyfriend wants me to', or, 'My husband says I am fat', or, 'I want to be as slim as my best friend', are common reflections shared with me. They often want the easy way out and look for quick-fix remedies, which then fail and make them feel worse. Morally dejected, they start another cycle of yo-yo dieting.

Exercise and clean eating needs to be a part of your life, not an isolated incident that happens occasionally in a vacuum. It should happen as naturally as brushing your teeth or taking a shower every day. Along with exercise and clean eating, staying productive is critical to staying focused without obsessing. There are millions of things you can do to stay busy. Hobbies, work and passions can be actively pursued. This prevents a preoccupation with food and weight. Your body will gradually change even if you are not scrutinizing it and criticizing it every single day. In the meantime, stay busy. Stay challenged in other ways. Help others make the change. There is nothing like helping others to make you feel good. If you have travelled that path of trying to get fit and lose weight in the right way and succeeded, inspire others to do the same. Do different things. Walk with a friend. Organize a dance party. Go on a trek. Take your kids on a picnic.

Keep moving forward, stay busy, enjoy solitude, love life, have a passion. Life is more than a number on the scale. Rather, it is about what we do with this short time we have on this earth.

ACKNOWLEDGEMENTS

A book never gets written in a vacuum. There have been innumerable contributions and influences from various quarters to finally make this a reality in print. I owe my deepest gratitude to everyone who has been involved with this book in any way possible.

I am thankful to Rupa Publications and Kapish Mehra for their continued support of my writing. My editor, Meenakshi Singh for answering my endless queries, sorting through my work and putting it together seamlessly. My copy editor, Sayan Das for all the work put in. To artist, Mohit Suneja who contributed the illustrations.

Shoba Krishnamoorthi, Kavitha Rao, DeviPrasad Rao, Padma Divarauni and Akhila Krishnamoorthi for your much-appreciated feedback after reading various parts of my work. Kanchana Manavalan and Nat for your support whenever I am in Madras. Nirmala Lakshman, Renuka Jaypal and Sharan Apparao for your valuable inputs every time we chat. B.J. Krishnan, Vanaja Krishnan, Nafeesa Begum, Raissa B. and late Col. Naidu for your belief in me. Shantha Ramachandran for easing my workload at the hospital. Anita Kumar, Queenmary Rajendran and Venita Pradeep my able assistants at the hospital, for making my life smoother. My amazing team of nurses, technicians, para-medical staff and help from various quarters at the hospital. Murugan Kasi, Durga Satishkumar, Martha Ashok and Vazeem for keeping the TFL Studio running like a well-oiled machine even in my absence.

My extensive circle of dear friends, you know who you all are, who have one way or another supported me and my writing with your encouragement, laughter, conversations, shared meals and much more.

I owe my deepest gratitude to my beloved, late father, Raghavan Nambiar for making me believe that anything is possible and my mother, Indira Nambiar for teaching me that anything is possible, provided one works very hard for it. You lead by example! Rekha Raghavan, Vinod Raghavan, Priya Baskar and Baskar Ethirajan for just being there for me. Sara, Rhea and Samar for bringing more sunshine into my life. Anjali Prabhu for your treasured friendship and all the thought provoking conversations we have had over the years. Poornima Giridhar for sharing with me some very rough and very fun times, especially through medical school and now, way beyond. Layak, for your endless inspiration and unwavering love, as always. For your keen criticism, (even though not always welcome!), profound wisdom and humor.

WOMEN WHO GAINED TO LOSE
Some Experiences

I was a cocktail of woes—obese, weak, with low energy levels; menopause was only the teeny, tiny pink paper umbrella that topped the cocktail. But all that changed when I started working out. Weight training has made me stronger. My arms and legs don't seem like they are controlled by an invisible master puppeteer and I no longer walk like I am on a continual whisky diet. Being fit makes me feel good about myself, and this is reflected in my thoughts and actions; relationships; in my work; in the way I dress etc.

— Jalaja Pillai

∾

It was a rude awakening when I was mobbed in Gudalur, mistaken for the CM, I knew I had to hit the gym. Following a fitness programme has worked wonders for my health and mental wellbeing.

— Meera Pothen

∾

Fitness has taught me patience, dedication and most of all 'heart'. I now have goals on my mind and am willing to do what it takes to reach them. I challenge myself everyday with dreams that help me grow in wisdom and strength and most of all, learn about myself. I am now a better person in all ways possible!

— *Nadia Saif*

∾

Exercising is about more than just weight loss. I am so much more energized and active. The racing heart and sore muscles are strangely satisfying.

Previously I was a cardio freak but now I've understood how important weight training, to build muscle and flexibly, is for holistic fitness. I am now more aware of what I eat and have stopped treating my stomach like a garbage bin. Life can only be lived to its fullest when one is fit and healthy.

— *Dr Ashwini Krishnamoorti*

∾

Physical fitness leads to mental balance, emotional well-being, the right attitude, the right outlook, and it puts the whole world in a new perspective. We started with just physical fitness, all else followed as by-products. The benefits I have derived from fitness are unexplainable. Today I am a fit person with abundant energy and an un-compromising outlook.

— *Dowlath Nisha*

∾

I learned that exercising right was more important than just 'exercising'. That building muscle was important and getting fit was a slow process, which needed commitment.

That it was okay to backslide but you had to get back on the saddle. I realized the importance of a good pair of shoes to prevent injury, the material to choose for workout clothes to prevent chaffing and the other little things that no one tells you about. I learnt the importance of warming up before the workout and stretching after the workout. I started feeling more energetic and confident in my own body. I could go shopping for clothes that fit and I didn't live in denial anymore. So now, when I don't work out or when I eat unhealthy I don't go on crazy crash diets. I get back on track. I am not perfect but I am OK with that. I am working towards being better and not adhering to the standards someone else sets.

— *Tanya Thimraj*

∿

One of the easiest things to do when you follow a tough exercise regimen is to give up halfway. Haven't we heard of the many stories where people buy an expensive gym membership but never end up working out? I was certain I didn't want to fall into that category. Now, I'm well on my way to getting fitter, better and healthier. My stamina, strength and flexibility have improved. Friends and family tell me that they see a marked difference in me. The words they use are 'happy, confident and positive'. That is so true. I feel happy, confident and full of energy. Now I feel like I can do anything that I want to! Did I mention, one of the (best) side-effects of starting to exercise is that I have lost thirteen kilos?

— *Dhivya Neelakandan*

∿

Like most women in Indian society, I put my husband and family first and took the back seat where my own wellness was concerned. I got my wake-up call one day in 2013, when I climbed on the scale. I was horrendously overweight, had swollen ankles, and was waddling around like a duck. I realized that I desperately needed to turn my life around and that is when I joined a fitness programme. The first few months were really tough. Muscles, I had never known existed, had woken up and were protesting violently. But, I was determined! Now, after nearly two years, I have become healthier, my aches and pains have disappeared and I have lost a ton of weight. Fitness has built up my confidence, helped me to make new friends, has improved my health and changed my view of life. For me, life began at 50 and I'm going to make the rest of my life the best of my life.

— *Rekha Peter*

∿

How time flies! Just the other day, I was slim and agile. So who is that person in the mirror—an unknown figure, plump and always in pain? My back hurt, I couldn't twist my neck while reversing the car and I couldn't see my toes, forget touching them. The less said about my memory the better. I had lists for lists! My bedside table began to resemble a mini-pharmacy—prescriptions, candy coloured pills, tubes of muscle relaxants, oils etc. My collection of X-rays and MRI scan reports steadily increased.

At my wit's end, I fixed an appointment with my fitness and lifestyle consultant. I was given a diet chart and started on a strength-training program for my back. I have not looked back since. I had doubts about whether

I would be able to do any of the exercises or lift weights, but these proved groundless. I feel so much better, stronger and healthier now after a year of weight training, stretches and cardio.

— *Aji Jaiprakash*

∾

Four years ago I was a perfunctory housewife with a tired look, sluggish gait and a constant crinkle of low self-esteem. I could have carried on this mundane existence, a life without fulfilment, an inert potential lying dormant within me never to be discovered.

Training has made me take responsibility of the well-being of my body. Other astonishing transformations came over me — better decision making skills, clarity in thinking, positivity, reversal of depression and anxiety, more confidence, less irritability, better management of stress and interpersonal skills. Best of all, a well-toned body . Physical exercise has brought a sense of psychological well-being to me, boosted my self-esteem and poise.

— *Mona Udayakumar*

∾

After two children and all the happiness showed in the amount of weight I had gained, one day I realized that I couldn't handle my own body weight. Finally, I made up my mind that it was about time I gave importance to my health. It took me time to get familiar with the exercises. I now know the importance of working out. Apart from becoming physically fit I have become more independent and more confident in facing life's challenges.

— *Shrutha Shankar*

BIBLIOGRAPHY

A. Belza et al. 'Contribution of Gastroenteropancreatic Appetite Hormones to Protein-Induced Satiety'. *American Journal Of Clinical Nutrition,* March 2013.

A. Misra et al. 'Obesity and Dyslipidemia in South Asians'. *Nutrients,* July 2013.

A. Misra et al. 'Obesity-related Non-communicable Diseases: South Asians vs White Caucasians'. *International Journal of Obesity,* February 2011.

A. Misra et al. 'The Metabolic Syndrome in South Asians: Epidemiology, Determinants, and Prevention'. *Metabolic Syndrome and Related Disorders,* December 2009.

A. Misra et al. 'Waist circumference cutoff points and action levels for Asian Indians for identification of abdominal obesity'. *International Journal of Obesity,* January 2006.

A. Scott et al. 'Ethnic Variation in Fat and Lean Body Mass and the Association with Insulin Resistance'. *Journal of Clinical Endocrinology and Metabolism,* May 2009.

A.D. Faigenbaum et al. 'Resistance Training Among Young Athletes: Safety, Efficacy and Injury Prevention Effects. *British Journal of Sports Medicine,* 2010.

A.D. Faigenbaum et al. 'State of the Art Reviews: Resistance

Training for Children and Adolescents. Are there Health Outcomes?' *American Journal of Lifestyle Medicine*, May 2007.

A.L. Iris et al. 'A Cross-Sectional Analysis of the Association between Physical Activity and Visceral Adipose Tissue Accumulation in a Multiethnic Cohort'. *Journal of Obesity*, August 2012.

A.R. Saltiel and C.R. Kahn. 'Insulin Signaling and the Regulation of Glucose and Lipid Metabolism'. *Nature*, December 2001.

Ahmad Afaghi et al. 'High Glycemic-index Carbohydrate Meals Shorten Sleep Onset'. *Am Jour Cli Nutrition*, February 2007.

B.V. Howard et al. 'Low-fat Dietary Pattern and Risk of Cardiovascular Disease: A Women's Health Initiative. Randomized Controlled Dietary Modification Trial'. *JAMA*, February 2006.

C. Weyer et al. 'Metabolic Factors Contributing to Increased Resting Metabolic Rate and Decreased Insulin-induced Thermogenesis during the development of Type 2 Diabetes'. *Diabetes*, August 2007.

C.G.R. Perry et al. 'High-intensity Aerobic Interval Training Increases Fat and Carbohydrate Metabolic Capacities in Human Skeletal Muscle'. *Journal of Applied Physiology, Nutrition, and Metabolism*, June 2000.

C.L. Melby et al. 'Effects of Acute Resistance Exercise on Post-exercise Energy Expenditure and Resting Metabolic Rate'. *Journal of Applied Physiology*, 1993.

Caitlin Mason et al. 'History of Weight Cycling Does Not Impede Future Weight Loss or Metabolic Improvements in Postmenopausal Women'. *Metabolism Clinical and Experimental*, June 2012.

D.A. Sedlock et al. 'Effect of Exercise Intensity and Duration on Post-exercise Energy Expenditure'. *Medicine and Science in Sports and Exercise,* June 1989.

D. Avery et al. 'The Effects of Different Resistance Training Protocols on Muscle Strength and Endurance Development in Children'. *Journal of American Academy of Pediatrics,* July 1999.

D.K. Layman, et al. 'Dietary Protein and Exercise have Additive Effects on Body Composition during Weight Loss in Adult Women'. *Journal Nutrition,* August 2005.

E. Kristen et al. 'Low-Carbohydrate Weight Loss Diets: Effects on Cognition and Mood'. *Appetite,* February 2009.

Ellen M. Evans et al. 'Effects of Protein Intake and Gender on Body Composition Changes: A Randomized Clinical Weight Loss Trial'. *Nutrition and Metabolism,* June 2012.

Eric C. Westman et al. 'Low-carbohydrate Nutrition and Metabolism'. *American Journal of Clinical Nutrition,* August 2007.

F. Ben et al. 'Strength Training as a Counter Measure to Aging Muscle and Chronic Disease'. *Journal of Sports Medicine,* April 2011.

G. Mastorakos. 'Exercise and the Stress System'. *Hormones,* April-June, 2005.

G.A. Bray et al. 'Effect of Dietary Protein Content on Weight Gain, Energy Expenditure, and Body Composition during Overeating: A Randomized Control Trial'. *JAMA,* January 2012.

H. Zouhal. 'Catecholamines and the Effects of Exercise, Training and Gender.' *Journal of Sports Medicine,* April 2013.

Henson et al. 'Associations of objectively measured sedentary behavior and physical activity with markers of cardiometabolic health'. *Diabetologia*, March 2013.

I. Tabata. 'Effects of Moderate-intensity Endurance and High-intensity Intermittent Training on Anaerobic Capacity and VO2max'. *Medicine and Science in Sports and Exercise,* October 1996.

J. Helgerud. 'Aerobic High-Intensity Intervals Improves VO2max more than Moderate Training'. *Medicine and Science in Sports and Exercise,* April 2007.

J. Laforgia et al. 'Comparison of Energy Expenditure Elevations after Sub-maximal and Supramaximal Running'. *Journal of Applied Physiology*, February 1997.

J. LaForgia et al. 'Effects of Exercise Intensity and duration on the Excess Post-exercise Oxygen Consumption'. *Journal of Sports Science,* December 2006.

J. Pinkney. 'The Role of Ghrelin in Metabolic Regulation'. *Current Opinion Clinical Nutrition Metabolic Care*, August 2014.

J.F. Horowitz and S. Klein. 'Lipid Metabolism during Endurance Exercise'. *American Journal of Clinical Nutrition,* February 2007.

J.L. Talanian et al. 'Two Weeks of High-intensity Aerobic Interval Training Increases the Capacity for Fat Oxidation During Exercise in Women'. *Journal of Applied Physiology,* April 2007.

James O. Prochaska et al. 'The Transtheoretical Model of Health Behavior Change'. *American Journal of Health Promotion Vol 12*, September 1997.

Jeff M. Reynolds, Len Kravitz. 'Resistance Training and

EPOC'. *IDEA Fitness Journal.*

K.A. Burgomaster et al. 'Similar Metabolic Adaptations during Exercise after Low Volume Sprint Interval and Traditional Endurance Training in Humans'. *Journal of Physiology,* January 2008.

K.J. Acheson. 'Diets for Body Weight Control and Health: The Potential of Changing the Macronutrient Composition'. *European Journal of Clinical Nutrition,* May 2013.

K.L. Osterberg and C.L. Melby. 'Effect of Acute Resistance Exercise on Postexercise Oxygen Consumption and Resting Metabolic Rate in Young Women'. *International Journal of Sport Nutrition and Exercise Metabolism,* September 2000.

Kimber L. Santhrope et al. 'Consuming Fructose Sweetened, not Glucose sweetened beverages, Increases Visceral Adiposity and Lipids and Decreases Insulin Sensitivity in Overweight/Obese Humans'. *Journal of Clinical Investigation,* April 2009.

Len Kravitz. 'Resistance Training: Adaptations and Health Implications'. *IDEA Fitness Journal,* 1996.

M. Gibala. 'Molecular Responses to High-intensity Interval Exercise'. *Applied Physiology, Nutrition, and Metabolism,* March 2009.

M.A. Burleson et al. 'Effect of Weight Training Exercise and Treadmill Exercise on Elevated Post-exercise Oxygen Consumption. *Medicine and Science in Sports and Exercise,* April 1998.

M.J. Bopp et al. 'Lean Mass Loss is Associated with Low Protein Intake during Dietary Induced Weight Loss in Post-menopausal Women'. *Journal of American Dietetic Association,* July 2008.

M.J. Muller et al. 'Is There Evidence for a Set-point that Regulates Human Body Weight?' *F1000 Medicine Reports*, August 2010.

M.S. Westerterp-Plantenga et al. 'Dietary Protein—Its Role in Satiety, Energetics, Weight Loss and Health'. *British Journal of Nutrition*, August 2012.

Martin J. Gibala et al. 'Short term Sprint Interval Versus Traditional Endurance Training. Similar Initial Adaptation in Human Skeletal Muscle and Exercise Performance'. *Journal of Physiology*, 2006.

Martin J. Gibala. 'Just HIT It! A Time Efficient Exercise Strategy to Improve Muscle Insulin Sensitivity. *Journal of Physiology*, September 2010.

McClemon et al. 'The Effects of a Low Carbohydrate Ketogenic Diet and a Low Fat Diet on Mood, Hunger and Other Self Reported Symptoms'. *Obesity*, January 2007.

Micah Zuhl and Len Kravitz. 'HIIT vs. Continuous Endurance Training: Battle of Aerobic Titans'. *IDEA Fitness Journal*, February 2012.

'Physical Activity for Young People'. *PCPFS Research Digest*, March 2010.

R. Bahr et al. 'Effect of Intensity of Exercise on Excess Post-Exercise Oxygen Consumption'. *Metabolism*, August 1991.

R. Wolfe. 'The underappreciated role of muscle in health and disease'. *American Journal of Clinical Nutrition 8*, September 2006.

R.B. Harris et al. 'Role of Set-point in Regulation of Body Weight'. *Federation of American Societies for Experimental Biology Journal*, December 1990.

R.J. Godfrey et al. 'The Exercise-induced Growth Hormone

Response in Athletes'. *Journal of Sports Medicine,* 2003.

R.L. Weinsier et al. 'Do Adaptive Changes in Metabolic Rate Favor Weight Regain in Weight-reduced Individuals. An examination of the Set-Point Theory'. *American Journal of Clinical Nutrition,* November 2000.

R.W. Haltomet et al. 'Circuit Weight Training and its Effects on Excess Post-exercise Oxygen Consumption'. *Medicine and Science in Sports and Exercise,* November 1999.

Renee Vogt et al. 'Psychological Effects of Weight Loss and Regain: A Prospective Evaluation'. *Journal of Consulting and Clinical Psychology,* August 1996.

Rhodri S. Lloyd et al. 'Position Statement on Youth Resistance Training: The 2014 International Consensus', *British Journal of Sports Medicine*, 2014.

S. Anoob et al. 'High body fat and low muscle mass are associated with increased arterial stiffness in Asian Indians in North India'. *Journal of Diabetes and its Complications,* June 2014.

S. Chamukkan et al. 'Cut-off Values for Normal Anthropometric Variables in Asian Indian Adults'. *Diacare,* May 2003.

S.H. Holt et al. 'A satiety index of common foods'. *European Journal of Clinical Nutrition,* September 1995.

S. Melov et al. 'Resistance Exercise Reverses Aging in Human Skeletal Muscle'. *Public Library of Science,* May 2007.

S. Soenen et al. 'Normal Protein Intake Is Required for Body Weight Loss and Weight Maintenance, and Elevated Protein Intake for Additional Preservation of Resting Energy Expenditure and Fat Free Mass'. *Journal of Nutrition,* February 2013.

Sanjay R. Patel et al. 'Association between Reduced Sleep and Weight Gain in Women. *American Journal of Epidemiology*, February 2006.

Scott et al. 'Osteoporosis and Strength Training'. *American Journal of Lifestyle Medicine*, August 2009.

Simone A. French et al. 'Consequences of Dieting to Lose Weight: Effects on Physical and Mental Health'. *Health Psychology*, May 1994.

Stephan Guyenet and Michael W. Schwartz. 'Regulation of Food Intake, Energy Balance and Body Fat Mass: Implications for the Pathogenesis and Treatment of Obesity. *Journal of Clinical Endocrinology and Metabolism*, March 2012.

Stephen H. Boutcher. 'High-intensity Intermittent Exercise and Fat loss'. *Journal of Obesity*, October 2010.

Timothy Noakes. *Waterlogged: The Serious Problem of Overhydration in Endurance Sports*. Human Kinetics, May 2012.

V.A. Convertino et al. 'Exercise and fluid replacement'. *American College of Sports Medicine Position Stand*, 1996.